About the Author

Chester is a young trans man from Hertfordshire, England. With an over active imagination, he has always used writing to bring the worlds and ideas in his head alive, even when he was still small and just learning to write! To have his words printed in books is a massive achievement that he's entirely honoured by.

An End's Beginning

Chester Prior

An End's Beginning

Olympia Publishers
London

First Published in 2023

Olympia Publishers
Tallis House
2 Tallis Street
London
EC4Y 0AB

Printed in Great Britain

Acknowledgements

Thank you to my family whose unwavering support in my life and everything I try to do has allowed me to achieve my dreams and write this book.

Chapter 1

He pulled his dog back around the side of the building. The dog resisted against the pull on his bandana collar, but the boy pulled harder, grabbing his scruff. The rumble of the tyres on the dirt and the rev of the engine made him sweat and his heart beat harder. They ducked down between two wooden boxes. There was a ragged tarpaulin laying over it which obscured them from the outside.

He clamped his hand over the dog's grey muzzle when he growled. "Shush, Briggs!" he snapped.

Through a rip in the plastic, he could see the car drive past.

Crude metal armour, patterned with a red stain, covered the car. The car had no roof. One of its riders was stood in the back holding onto the metal roll bar. Two people jumped out. Two shirtless men, wearing tattered trousers and heavy boots. Both had the same red line pattern painted on their chests. They walked into a smaller building and after a short while emerged with a few items in their hands. One returned to the car whilst the other looked back through the door.

The boy's heart pounded as he willed them to leave. The explosion made him grab onto Briggs tighter. The dog jumped as well, pinning his ears to the back of his head. He could see the edge of the blue blast through the holes and the man running back to the car, cackling. His comrades shouting at him for 'doing it again', before they sped away into the horizon.

9

They stayed where they were, his hands wrapped around his dog's body. The boy closed his eyes for a moment to calm his trembling down. They had been inches from death. If they had come around to this building, to the door that was metres away from them, then he would have died.

Briggs fidgeted, he let the dog go. Briggs never strayed very far, he always waited for his companion to follow. With a dry swallow and a deep exhale, he stood and climbed out of their hiding place.

Curiosity got the better of him when he looked to the charred remains of the little building. He wandered over. Briggs let out a long growl that ended in a bark when he got too close. "I know, I know. 'Don't go near that, Ren'," he spoke in a deeper voice that sounded like an old man, because that's how he thought Briggs would sound. "I'm only looking at it, I'm not going to go in."

Ren had seen this weapon before. He didn't actually have any idea what it was or how it did what it did, but he knew its impact. It looked like a small grenade, that they would throw. When it hit the ground, it released a huge bright blue dome. Long branches of white blue electricity would come from the centre, burning everything that was inside. It was terrifying to see it reduce the building to a blackened mess in moments.

As Ren peered through the door, parts of the roof fell inwards. They crashed to the ground and broke into ashy pieces. Briggs barked again. Ren looked over at him; his brown head was low, his eye trained on Ren. His white and brown, patchy legs were wide in a defensive stance and the black hairs across his back stood on end.

Ren raised his hands and he stepped away from the building. "Okay, I'm coming," he said to his dog. Briggs stood a little straighter and the white tip of his tail wagged twice. He licked Ren's hand when he lowered it to pet him. "At least we know we're going the right way now. We've seen quite a lot of them lately, the Raider base must be around here somewhere," Ren said, looking off in the direction the car had driven. "I hope we can find her."

Chapter 2

Ren adjusted the satchel on his back, it was starting to feel heavy again. His feet were getting sore but their destination was on the horizon. They were walking down a long stretch of road, the white markings having long worn off, but the asphalt was still intact for the most part. One of the only reminders of the past times that still protruded from the dusty wastelands of today. Nothing stood on either side of the road, except for the odd dead tree, rock or metal post.

Briggs trotted alongside him, sniffing at the ground or the air now and again. Ren wondered how much more of the world he could discover if he had the nose of a dog. It would have been a hell of a lot easier to find *Her* if he could have followed the scent. Briggs wasn't a tracking dog so he couldn't have followed the scent. Nor would they have been able to keep up before the scent went cold anyway, so he most definitely didn't hold a grudge against Briggs for that. Ren was glad he wasn't making the journey alone or he would have gone mad by now. The blazing sun had a talent for doing that to people.

The tall stone walls approached, the people standing guard becoming distinct shapes now. This was North Bridge. Ren didn't understand why that was its name. There was a lot more to the North of it and it bridged nothing but he didn't care enough, when they told him to ask. It was nothing more than a pit stop.

They approached the guards at the front gates of the

walled town. They had dusty guns in their hands and a thin cloth covered their heads and faces to protect them from the sun.

"State your business," the first guard said.

"I'm here for supplies," Ren answered just as shortly.

"You a wanderer?" he asked.

"No, just passing by," Ren said.

"Ya got money?" the second guard spoke up.

"Obviously." Ren frowned and raised his eyebrow.

"Fine. Eyes and tongue," the first guard ordered.

Ren lowered his sunglasses and stuck out his tongue. The guard lent a little closer to look and then he peered down at Briggs. His bright pink tongue was hanging out as he panted. The guard nodded his head towards the gates. They pulled it open for Ren to enter.

"Welcome to North Bridge," he said before closing the door behind Ren.

North Bridge was a ghost town, metaphorical and literal. The front gates opened up into what would have once been a town square in the old world. A dried-up fountain stood in the middle. Its outer bowl broken in many places so it could no longer hold water. Around the edges of the 'square' were the new streets.

Unrefined buildings stood in wobbly rows making up the roads. They housed the people who never adjusted or the ones who had 'useful' jobs. Sheltering people like doctors and builders from the harsh weathers and creatures outside.

They turned down a street, it was void of people but there was a tap sticking up out of the ground. It had a tax clamp on the handle. Ren tried to turn it in the hope that someone had turned it off before their money had run out. It didn't budge, of course. Ren rolled his eyes. Money had no value any more, so he was going to push the pointless circles of metal into this slot to get some water. It was a futile way to keep what little control the authorities could.

Ren crouched and dug through his satchel, finding the two glass bottles he kept on him. There was a little left in one of them. He pulled out Briggs's water dish – which was in fact an old car hub cap – and tipped the remaining water in it. Then, he found some coins that fit inside the slot on the tax clamp. The coins slid down into the small metal container underneath. Ren could hear the pressure in the pipe build. He positioned the bottle first before opening the tap. The water poured out. Ren tried to ignore that it was a little cloudy still, but he'd drunk a lot worse and it hadn't killed him yet.

He filled his bottles just as the pressure in the tap became weak, before it stopped completely. Briggs licked up the final drips, wasting nothing.

They packed up and wandered off further into the town in search of food. The smell caught Ren's attention first. Then the buzzing of the flies around the hanging carcasses. The meat was behind the shop window, but the smell still drifted out the open door. A wooden countertop stopped Ren from entering. The butcher appeared in front of him, wiping his bloody hand on a rag. "I'll have whatever's freshest," Ren said. The butcher nodded and turned away taking a carcass out of the window and chopping it up on a table in the back of the shop. Briggs licked his lips when the butcher approached with Ren's ration wrapped in brown paper. Ren handed over some more pointless coins. "Thank you, stay safe," Ren said as he turned away. The butcher smiled one-sidedly and tossed Briggs a chunk of tough fat, his favourite part of any meal.

Ren sat on the remains of the fountain in the square letting Briggs chew his gift. He'd overheard why the town was more dead than expected. There was a sand storm on its way and people were bunkering down ready for it. That was not ideal. Sand storms were dangerous for obvious reasons. More so to Ren because he really didn't want to get blown off course. He'd just found a lead of sorts; seeing those Raiders earlier meant he was going in the right direction. He didn't need to be getting lost in a sandstorm and end up backtracking at all. He hoped he'd be able to find some sort of shelter before it caught up with them.

They left the walled city shortly. Ren had his supplies and Briggs had had a meal so there was no point hanging around. They walked around the sides of North Bridge and looked out across the barren horizon. Ren dug through his bag and pulled out a small leather box. He flipped open the lid, being careful of its splitting sides. Under a glass dome the needle wobbled about over the compass face. He wiped the dirt off the glass and tucked the compass back in his bag. They continued on, still heading the right way.

***

A city appeared on the horizon. An old city, from the world before. It was barely standing; only some of the buildings still scraped the sky. Ren weaved around cars that had found their final resting place in the original panic. Rusting and decaying. He looked at the rotting buildings, the naked rebars stretching out like a sick imitation of trees. Ren hadn't seen a living tree in months, or was it years now?

They came across a corner shop. Briggs sniffed hard

under the door; his breaths amplified by the wood. Ren wouldn't often search a place like this. Most of the food, medication or anything somewhat useful already looted out of it. But Briggs was scratching to get in. Ren trusted his dog.

He felt along the back of his trousers, double checking his pocket knife was in there, before he jerked the door open. He peaked around the door, making sure no one was hiding in there. The coast was clear and he let Briggs trot in.

It was dusty and dark inside. Nothing left on the shelves. Briggs expertly hopped over a broken bottle and disappeared behind the till. There was a door that perhaps led to some sort of back room. Ren could hear him taking long breaths under that door as well. Ren tried the handle but it was locked. Briggs scratched at the door frame.

Ren let his head roll back on his shoulders for a minute as he contemplated whether this was worth the effort. If there wasn't anything in there it could at least be a safe place to hide.

"Move over," Ren said, pushing Briggs to the side. He braced himself against the counter behind him. He lifted his foot and kicked the door as hard as he could. He heard the wood splinter. Again, he forced his foot to the door. He sighed heavily; it was almost there. Once more should do it. With the final kick the door broke open.

Ren opened the door with caution, as always. He took a step in before letting Briggs come in.

His stomach dropped and his throat tightened. He shut his eyes, trying to stop himself from throwing up, but the smell in the room twisted his stomach. He blocked Briggs with his leg when he felt him step forwards.

After regaining control of his breathing, Ren opened his eyes. He looked at the corpse sat next to a pile of tin cans.

Their shop uniform hung off their bones. There was a name tag pinned to their chest pocket but Ren couldn't bring himself to read it. He didn't want their soul following him as well.

Ren looked down to Briggs, who was sat behind him. He signalled him to stay with his open palm. Briggs lowered his head as he watched Ren walk further into the room. Ren grimaced when the soles of his canvas shoes stuck slightly to the tacky floor. He stopped his mind from figuring out what was causing it.

Slowly, he sifted through the cans, picking some of the unopened ones and packing them into his bag. His bag was pretty full already, so he only took a few. He told himself, this was the reason he only took a few and not the feeling that he was disturbing a tomb.

He straightened up and walked to the doorway. He turned once more before he left, bowed his head and said, "Thank you, you've been a great help to us. Now please rest peacefully." Ren pulled the door closed again and they left the shop quietly.

***

Wind whipped around the streets; it blew Ren's hood up the back of his head. Briggs had his ears pinned closed behind his head and his eyes squinted to stop the dirt going in. Ren looked up at the building next to them. It was some sort of office building, and there weren't many obvious holes in it. Ren pushed at the heavy glass door; Briggs slid in the gap quickly. He huffed aloud, echoing Ren's own relief to be out of that wind.

"Well, guess we'll stay here for tonight," Ren said to his

dog. "Come on let's have a look around."

They wandered through the foyer; everything seemed pretty intact. Either the wind that whipped through the broken windows had trashed the place, or people had. It wasn't a complete wreck. They passed the front desk and the plants, hanging brown over the side of their pots. There were some stairs ahead. Ren liked to be on the upper floors, overlooking the streets.

The offices were all the same, nothing of any interest left in any of them. There was a small hole in the side of the building, the roof of the next building a small leap across from them. Ren found a corner office and set his bag down. This one had a large leather sofa in it, a perfect bed for the night. Glass made up the two external walls, looking out over the remains of the city.

The red and oranges of the sky would have been beautiful before. Now all Ren could see them as was: radioactive. The same was true of the blistering sun, that never seemed to give any respite after *that* day.

It hadn't started how everyone had thought it would. People joked about 'World War 3' a lot. Every time there was a little tension between two countries, people made fun of it on the internet. They thought nothing would come of it. Ren had thought that as well. And it didn't happen how they'd thought it would either. Instead of people going to fight for their motherland, the rich gave the order to send their weapons.

Instead of it lasting months or years, cities were gone in days. Thousands lost, because of human greed.

Briggs whined. Ren looked into his brown eyes, they glowed in the golden sunset. Ren opened his bag and dug one of the cans out. It didn't have a label. Ren cracked the pull tab open and emptied the contents onto the floor. A pile of mixed vegetables poured out. Briggs licked it up regardless. Ren tossed him a chunk of meat as well and laid his dish down, filling it with water. They ate together in silence. Ren opening his own tin can, once again thanking the person they had found them with. Even though he hadn't looked at their name he felt as if their soul would follow him anyway.

Darkness filled the room. Ren called Briggs onto the sofa with him. Briggs laid down between his legs, his head resting on Ren's stomach. Ren stroked his soft ears as he tried to fall asleep. When Briggs started to snore, Ren felt himself relax. He wouldn't be asleep if there was danger about.

Chapter 3

A gun shot echoed out behind Ren making him quicken his pace. He clutched his bag tight to his chest as he ran through the city's streets. A building in front of him was on fire.

The glass from a shop front exploded out at him. He fell to the floor, his eyes wide and petrified. The person in the shop turned and continued swinging his crowbar at the various electronic items on the shelves. Ren scrambled off the floor and ran away. He skidded around corners and ducked into alleyways to avoid the people who were tearing around in a car. He crossed the road right as the car crashed full speed into a brick wall a little up the road from him. Ren stared for a moment, but the people didn't emerge from it as smoke rose from the bonnet. He shook his head and continued running; that wasn't his problem to deal with.

The shouts, gunfire and car sounds died down as he ran into the forest. He allowed himself to take a breath as the familiar, thick shrubs obscured him. His step was light and quiet as he reached the house. He looked up at the curtains, still closed in all the windows, and the doors still shut tight. Ren snuck around the back, silently. He looked through the trees around him. Seeing no unfamiliar figures, he pushed the door handle down, relieved to feel the slight resistance of the deadbolt first. The sound of claws crossing the wood floor greeted him. Ren turned from closing the door and smiled as Briggs approached, wagging his tail.

"Flo?" he asked into the silence. Ren climbed the stairs, Briggs following close behind.

Ren traversed the dark house, crossing the landing to the last room at the end. He creaked the door open and smiled. Yellow candlelight filled the small room. A child's writing table stood in the centre. Flo lay slumped over it, crayon still in hand, sound asleep. Ren slid in the doorway. Pushing the tiny dresser – he always told Flo to put there while he was out – out of the way. Briggs sniffed at Flo's sleeping face but then left her and curled up in his basket. Ren dragged the wardrobe in place of the dresser, over the door. He winced when it scraped along the floor but turned to see Flo still sleeping. Ren placed the bag of food he'd managed to find by their two plates on the floor in the corner.

Ren lifted Flo up, taking a brief look at the drawing she was doing of them both holding hands. He took her to the little child's bed and laid down with her held close to his chest. She pressed her head against his chin, the tight curls of her hair tickling his face. He pushed them down, just for them to bounce straight back up again. He left his hand on her head as he stared up at their makeshift blanket fort. They'd laid blankets over a chest of drawers and an airer he'd found in the cupboard downstairs. It obscured them from the windows and the door should he have forgotten to close either of them.

Ren shook his head. They couldn't stay here much longer. He'd struggled to find food earlier and the streets were getting more dangerous. It'd only be a matter of time before the people started coming this way to find stuff to steal. Plus, he was certain he'd heard a monster growling outside the night before. He'd tried to convince himself his mind was playing tricks on him, but then he'd heard people in the city talking about things called 'mutants'. He certainly didn't want to find out what one of those was. They needed to get away from the city, to a quieter place. It had been months and he'd stayed only in the hopes that their grandparents would come back. At this point Ren was sure that they wouldn't. It was too dangerous on the streets of the city for two old people, that's if they even survived that shockwave.

Ren shook his head to stop the tears from falling from his eyes. He didn't need to be crying in front of Flo.

He'd decided. They were going to leave as soon as Flo woke again. He slid her off of him and left her in bed. He silently gathered their things, packing them into his satchel. He moved the wardrobe and scavenged around the house for anything else that could be of use to them. When he got back, Flo was awake, making a sickness rise in his stomach.

"What're you doing?" she asked groggily.

"We're going to leave," Ren answered her honestly.

"Why?" she asked.

"Because…" Ren paused thinking of an answer. "We're going to find a castle to live in."

"Really?" Her eyes glowed at him.

"Yeah, but we'll only be able to find one if you listen to me really well."

"I will," she said seriously, "but only if when we get there, I get to be the princess and you can be a knight!"

"Why do I have to be a knight? Why can't I be a prince as well?" Ren smiled at her usual enthusiasm.

"Because, brothers don't get to be princes. They have to be knights," she said matter of fact.

"Right, right. I get it." Ren laughed a little.

"What about Nana and Grandad?" Her voice changed to

concern.

Ren tightened his jaw and busied himself with their bags. "They'll meet us there."

"How will they know where to go?"

"The Royal Messenger will go get them." Ren turned, plastering a smile on his face.

"Oh yes!" Flo said, like it was obvious.

Ren grabbed some warmer clothes for her and helped her into them. He was gentle as he pulled her hair into two bunches on either side of her head. They looked uneven and lumpy but it'd be better than it getting in her face. Ren dressed himself and then pulled Flo's purple raincoat on her. "Right, let's go." Ren smiled to her.

"Okay!" she called back, jumping a little on the spot.

They went downstairs and to the back door, where three pairs of welly boots stood in a line. Ren helped Flo climb into hers and then grabbed Briggs's slip lead off the hook by the door. He wagged his tail when Ren slipped it around his neck.

"Right, you have to be really quiet, okay?" Ren said, crouching to Flo's level.

"Aye aye, Captain!" She saluted like a soldier. Ren returned a curt nod.

He pulled open the door and peered outside. It looked clear. Ren wrapped Briggs's lead tighter around his hand and then grabbed Flo's. Ren's heart was in his throat as they stepped out together and walked away from the house.

"Aren't you gonna shut the door?" Flo whispered.

"No, no one's coming back here," Ren said, eyes fixed in front of him.

Chapter 4

Briggs jumped from Ren's lap, waking him in an instant. His mind struggled to fight through the fog of sleep. He found Briggs's shape in the darkness. He was sniffing under the door quietly, then he trotted over to the window. He let out a low growl. The hairs on his back stood, silhouetted against the early morning light. Ren stood and snuck along the office wall until he could see down to the street.

There were three Raider cars parked on the street. They were entering the building next door and the one across the street.

Briggs's claws clicked against the floor as he ran back to the door. A laugh echoed down the hallway and turned Ren's stomach. He ran back to their stuff, shoving everything back into his bag. He threw it on his back and pulled his pocket knife out. He opened the blade and reached for the door handle.

The door opened before he could grab the handle and he jumped back. Briggs growled deep within his throat, baring his teeth at the figures in the doorway. Her features were dark in the strange light. "Hiding in our territory, ay?" the man behind her said.

"Don't worry, we'll skin ya once yer dead." As the woman spoke Briggs lunged at her, knocking her into the man. They both crashed down to the floor. Ren jumped over them and ran up the hall. He looked back for his dog. Briggs thrashed the Raider's arm in his mouth; he lifted his free hand to strike the dog.

"Brigadier!" Ren shouted. Briggs let the Raider go and ran after Ren before he could get hit.

Ren could barely hear them shouting after him over the sound of his footsteps on the floor. They skidded around the cubicles. He couldn't go down the stairs or he'd have to fight at least two more pairs. They ran through the last doorway. The sand and dirt blew past the hole in the wall. Ren's heart pounded; his throat was tight.

A loud shout from the female Raider forced Ren forwards. He sped towards the gap and jumped. The wind knocked him and his body slammed against the side of the building. The shadow of Briggs flew over him, he landed and rolled over onto his back. Ren pulled himself up onto the roof. Briggs waited for him and then turned to run just ahead of Ren jumping the gaps between the buildings. If an old dog could do it, so could he.

A length appeared between them and their assailants. Ren was small and quicker than they were in their heavy leather boots. He felt a little giddy, he could outrun them, and then hide until they gave up on finding him. That was, until he saw that bloodcurdling blue flash in the backs of his eyes.

It threw him across the wasteland, away from the rotting city. For a moment, he could see Briggs's body being flung in another direction. He didn't know if he was okay, he lost consciousness before he could even contemplate it.

Chapter 5

Ren jolted awake. In the same breath he winced as pain shot through his body. He exhaled slowly, steadying his breathing so as not to aggravate whatever was hurting him. He ran his palm over his ribs, nothing hurt there. He guessed it was his back. He opened his eyes again, squinting in the candle-light of the room. The walls were fabric, two candlesticks stood in the corners of the room. Ren shut his eyes again. His head was pounding. The bed he was laying on was hard and rough but the animal hides on top of him were soft and warm.

He sensed motion to his left and opened his eyes. A man was in the doorway, his hand holding the fabric door open. Ren tried to sit up, to do anything to protect himself. The man raised his hand as he entered.

"I'm not going to hurt you, kid." His voice was quiet and hoarse. Ren's heart still thumped in his chest as he tried to believe him.

The fact he was still alive, and in a bed, instead of a cage, told him that much.

"You had a pretty nasty encounter with them Raiders, eh?" he said eyeing Ren. The man hobbled forwards, leaning heavy on his walking stick. Ren flinched when he reached out towards him. But he only placed his hand on Ren's forehead.

"You've not got a fever and you seem pretty awake now. Hopefully, you haven't got an infection," he said more to himself than Ren.

The man reached into a wooden chest that stood next to the bed. He pulled out some lengths of rag and clear liquid in a bottle. Then he walked around the end of Ren's bed. Ren tried to lift his head to see what was happening. He lifted the covers off of Ren's leg and then he felt the man unwrap something off it. "This will sting," the man said, as he dumped some of the clear liquid onto the wound that was there. Ren hissed through his teeth, which in turn hurt his back causing him to cough dryly.

As his wound was re-dressed, Ren began to wake up properly. "Is it bad?" Ren asked, his throat sore and dry.

"Hmm, to be honest, I've never seen anyone survive a Blue Bolt," the man said. "But somehow, you've come off pretty well. It's superficial overall."

Ren nodded. "My dog? Did you see him at all?"

The old man looked up at him, his eyebrow raised. "A brown and white one?"

"Yeah, he's got a green bandana on," Ren said, unable to stop himself from smiling.

"Yeah, he came limping over, about an hour after you fell through our roof." The man stood and walked back to the box beside Ren.

He put the items away and then pulled the crate away from the wall and sat a little way from Ren. "Is he okay?" he asked the burning question first.

"Yeah, he's got some cuts and scrapes and he's reluctant to put full weight on his front paw but he's very much feeling okay. He hasn't exactly been easy to handle," the man said, dragging his fingers through his white beard.

"He's just protective," Ren said, defending his companion. The man hummed his answer.

"Who are you?" Ren asked.

"We're the Opal Fox Clan. We control the Central Regions," he explained.

"Except that city over there, I guess," Ren said.

The man smirked. "No, you would have been safe if we controlled that city. There's nothing in it though, so we don't want it."

Ren nodded again.

"I'm guessing you've not heard of us then?" the man said.

"No, I've only just crossed into this region," Ren answered.

"A wanderer, are you?"

"No... not exactly."

"What are you doing wandering about then?" The man lent forwards. A round, green gemstone hanging from a worn piece of string slipped out from the robe he was wearing. It was carved into the shape of a fox's head.

"I'm looking for some...thing," Ren answered, cautiously.

"Hmm, you don't like talking much, do you?" the man said.

"Guess not." Ren looked away. "I just want to get back on my way."

The man nodded sitting back up straight. "Gin wants to talk with you first, but rest for now. I can't promise you anything, but he might help you. At the least, we'll heal you, but we might have information of value to you." The man stood and pushed the box back to the wall. He turned to leave.

"Why are you helping me?" Ren shouted after him. The man stopped.

"I don't know. I can't ever tell what Gin is thinking," he

answered before leaving Ren by himself again.

Ren looked up at the ceiling. His head was spinning. The fact that he had been inches from death, again, hit him. Tears filled his eyes; he was so close to failing *her*. He lifted his right hand out from beneath the covers. He straightened the grey bandana on his wrist; *she* had a pink one. This was a setback, but he hoped that this Gin person was kind, and could point him in the right direction.

***

Ren had drifted off, when the old man returning woke him up again. "Gin wants to speak with you now," he said.

Two taller men entered behind him. They wore thin clothes and had metal armour pieces fastened to their chests, arms and legs. The old man helped him sit up. Ren now saw the bloody bandages wrapped around his left leg. It made him feel sick.

"Come on, lad," the man said, helping him stand.

The stronger men stood either side of Ren, taking most of his weight. His back hurt when they placed his arms over their shoulders, but it hurt less than the pain in his leg.

The old man led the way. They walked down the tent-like hallways, wooden and metal beams holding the fabric up. The fabrics were of all different colours. Some flapped hard in the wind and others only bowed against it. Ren couldn't keep track of where they were going, the journey was too long and the halls looked too similar. Two tall, burning torches stood either side of an opening in the right wall. They ducked into the room.

The room was massive, the ceiling high and held up by

tall wooden logs. People lined the walls, they all watched as Ren entered with the old man. In front of them was the leader. He sat on a great wooden throne, animal hides laying over the seat. He lounged back, his hand rested on his chin and a smile on his face as Ren was brought in. He was wearing a lightweight metal chest plate, the clan's insignia embossed onto the front. His long, light hair tied behind his head. His eyes were intense and fixed on Ren. The men carrying Ren, placed him on the floor a little way in front of the man.

A whine from the corner of the room distracted Ren from the leader. Briggs was laying on the floor, his ear pricked forwards. There were two clan members holding onto ropes around his neck, pulling him down to the floor. He fidgeted and struggled against the ropes, getting frustrated and angry.

"Stop, Briggs," Ren said quietly. He settled.

Ren looked back to the leader; he was watching him interact with his dog. Ren noticed he was holding something in his hand, panic rose in him.

"Be careful with that!" he called to the leader.

The man looked at the small rigid, leather case in his hand. "I was wondering where you'd gotten this. Seems pretty fancy for a kid to have," the leader said, his voice deep and powerful.

"It's mine! And it's fragile," Ren raised his voice.

The leader opened it; Ren could see the leather splitting as he looked at the inside. "A compass is a convenient thing to just have."

"Hence why I'm not dead yet." Ren scowled at him.

"Where'd you come from?" he asked Ren, closing the compass and putting it back with the rest of Ren's stuff at his feet.

"South."

"How far South?" The man lent forwards in his chair.

"Further than Land's End and the Southern Peak," Ren answered.

The leader's eyes widened a little. "You came all that way? On foot? With a dog?" Ren nodded.

"Why?" The man rested his elbows on his knees.

"I'm looking for someone."

"Who?"

"It doesn't matter to you," Ren said, his scowl deepening at all the questions.

The leader sat back. "Fine. What got you licked by a Blue Bolt?"

"We were camping in that city. I didn't know Raiders controlled it. They chased us out and we were getting away," Ren answered.

The man sat in silence. He sat back in his chair and stared into the middle distance, his hand idly kneading the back of his neck.

"What's your name?" he asked.

"Ren."

"Well Ren. I'm Gin, the Opal Fox leader, and I've decided that you can stay with us until you've healed up a bit. We might be able to find your missing person," Gin added.

"Why?" Ren asked, echoing the question he'd asked the old man before.

"Because, not just anyone comes that distance on their own, and survives an encounter with the Raiders. You might be of some use to us," Gin answered in truth.

Ren nodded at the ground. "Can I have my dog back now?" he asked, feeling drained and tired. Gin shrugged and nodded to the people holding Briggs back.

He bounded over as best he could, hopping on his front paw, the other holding up. He butted his head into Ren when he finally got to him. Ren scratched him all over, happy that he was okay and wagging his tail happily. He held his head still so he could look at him. Briggs licked his face and Ren smiled at him.

Briggs had a small cut running up his muzzle and between his eyes. Ren took hold of his paw. He pulled it away from Ren, but let him look in the end. A bandage was wrapped snug around it, Ren flexed it slightly both ways. Briggs licked Ren's hand and he let it go. It didn't seem broken, he hoped that he'd only sprained it a little.

"You can take him back now," Gin said to the men that had brought Ren there. Briggs snarled at them as they approached.

"AH!" Ren snapped at the dog. "They're helping me," he said softly. Briggs let them approach and he followed slowly behind them as they took Ren back to his bed. Ren's back cried from the stress of moving about, but the pain faded when he lay back down. Briggs jumped on to the bed and laid beside him. His tail swept along the bed when Ren petted his head. Ren's eyes were heavy, but he felt calm and safe for the first time in a very long time. Briggs was okay, and he was in a safe place, surrounded by people that might be able to help him.

Chapter 6

Ren was sat up in bed the next day. The old man had told him to sit up or he'd get sick from laying down. It hurt his back but he'd rather deal with a little soreness than die from a preventable sickness. Briggs's head lifted off Ren's leg and he huffed a bark towards the door. Moments later the fabric door opened. It surprised Ren to watch Gin duck through the doorway. "I've brought your things back," he said, placing Ren's satchel by his bed. "I've donated the food you had to the kitchen, seeing as you'll be hanging about for a little while. Obviously, when you choose to go again, we'll re-stock you."

Ren nodded. "Thanks."

"I've also got this for you," Gin said, holding out his hand. Ren took the item from him. It was his compass.

"I had our leather guy look at it. Seeing as it was barely holding together," Gin said.

Ren looked over the new leather casing, it was soft and neatly pulled over the wooden frame. The metal outer framing, shiny and polished. He'd never seen it like this. It was old before it was even given to them. He couldn't express how it made him feel, or how grateful he was.

"You didn't need to waste his time doing that," Ren said.

"Nah, I s'pose not, but it seemed to matter a lot to you. And no one's armour has needed repairing lately so…you know." Gin shrugged.

Ren just looked at him for a minute. He hadn't devoted

any time to taking in what this man looked like yesterday. He was very classically handsome; strong cheek bones and jaw; sharp, light-brown eyes; long, silver-blond hair that was balled up, behind his head. His body was well built and strong, skin tanned by the sun. Today he had the same metal chest piece on, but underneath he was wearing a navy-blue, long-sleeved shirt.

Gin lingered, somewhat awkwardly.

"This isn't what I imagined meeting a clan leader would be like. I thought you were all ruthless and scary," Ren said bluntly, going back to inspecting his compass.

"Who says I'm ruthless?" Gin asked, smirking.

"No one. Just assumed. Figured you'd have to be, to lead a clan," Ren said, looking up at him.

"I can be, but you seem like you've been through it so I'm going easy on you." Gin winked at Ren. Ren couldn't help smiling a little at his strange charm.

"Why thank you, you're too kind."

Gin lent against one of the wooden support beams. "I'm curious."

"About what exactly?" Ren asked.

"Just you," Gin said, looking away for a moment. "You look quite young and you've come so far on your own. You've crossed the Raiders and you came out alive. Not just anyone can do that."

"Twice. And it was dumb luck both times… Well, the first time they weren't coming for me," Ren mumbled.

"I'm curious about that as well. If you don't mind me asking," Gin said, his tone softening.

Ren turned the compass over in his hands. He placed it by his pillow and his hand moved to silk Briggs's ear.

"They took her and only her because she was smaller than me." Ren started. "We were looking for shelter. Someone had told us about a walled city giving shelter to kids. I figured we'd both get in because she was young and I was her brother. But the Raiders found us before we could get there." Ren stopped. Briggs licked his other hand.

"Why did they take her?" Gin asked.

"I don't know... I'd never even heard of the Raiders, didn't even know who they were until I heard someone talking about them later on... I didn't stand a chance. There were six against me," Ren explained. "Briggs tried but he's not a guard dog. He'd never shown aggression in his entire life but he tried his best to stop them anyway."

Ren finally looked back up at Gin. He was staring at the floor, his eyes ablaze and his face twisted. "They took a child? Those sick f—" Gin stopped himself. He took a deep breath, letting his anger subside. "You did what you could, both of you. Like I said, few people survive an encounter with them. They're ruthless and don't think twice about killing to get what they want."

The corners of Ren's mouth dragged down. The images of that day were filling his head again. He tried his hardest not to think about it, because he couldn't do anything to change it now, but the thoughts, and what ifs still crushed his soul.

Ren blinked the tears away to stop them from falling.

"Do you know where their base is?" Ren's voice was tiny.

"You want to go and confront them head on?" Gin raised his eyebrows at Ren.

"I can't think of anything else to do," Ren said, "I've never known what else to do." The tears came now, the hopelessness of it all.

"I'll help you," Gin said all of a sudden, "You certainly can't do it on your own but you might be able to do it with a clan."

Ren looked up at him. "I don't want this clan to get involved in my issues. What if they die?"

"They'd die fighting for a noble cause. Getting rid of the Raiders would do everyone good. The entire wasteland would be free of one less threat."

Ren didn't know what to say.

"But you need to heal up first. So, you can be a help to us." Gin smiled with sincerity.

"What do you want me to do in the meantime? I can't just stay here without pulling my weight some," Ren said.

"You'll come in handy. If nothing else, your knowledge of the wasteland to the South will be helpful," Gin said.

Gin pushed off of the post he was leaning on. "I'll leave you be. Ru will probably come to tend your wounds again soon. Just don't sweat it, chill while you can. We'll do some digging for you." Gin smiled to him.

"Is Ru the name of the old guy?" Ren asked.

"Yeah, I'm not surprised he didn't introduce himself." Gin grinned, thinking of his old friend. "I'll see you around."

Gin left, leaving Ren a little shellshocked. He'd been here one day and this man was already ready to risk his clan's lives to help him. Ren shook his head.

"I think he's a little mad," he said to Briggs. Briggs rolled onto his side and stretched his paws out. "You don't care, do you? You're just happy to be sleeping on a bed." Ren was relieved as well; he was happy his sense of security wasn't false and that these people seemed genuine.

***

As Gin had suspected, Ru appeared later on in the day. He had a bowl of stew in his hand, offering it to Ren.

"Made from your rations. You found some good stuff on your travels," Ru said, bending to open the wooden crate. "How's your leg, after walking on it yesterday?"

"It's okay, feels hot," Ren answered in between bites.

"That's expected," Ru answered, kneeling in front of Ren.

Ren watched him unwrap the bandage. The wound started on his calf, a single point of impact; the individual forks wrapping around to the front. Each slice was deep and surrounded by a thick red line. It wasn't weeping, only burnt and angry.

"You got off lucky, lad. Must have just caught you with a single fork or it would've torn your leg clean off," Ru said, applying a balm to the wounds.

"I didn't even feel it. Just the shockwave," Ren said. He grimaced at the cold balm when it touched his hot skin. "Thank you for looking after it."

"It's fine. My job is to keep everyone alive around here."

"Are you like, their doctor then?" Ren asked, hoping to get to know more about this place.

"I was a doctor before all this mess. If I can continue to help people, I will," Ru answered.

"Does everyone here have a job?"

"Everyone helps where they can. Some don't have skills from their past that can be useful but they find other ways to help out. I imagine you don't have many life skills either?"

Ren was taken aback by that comment.

"Not to be rude, lad. You seem too young to be a doctor

37

or something like that, I mean. But an extra pair of hands is always useful, regardless," Ru added, trying to seem less abrasive.

"I get it. And you're right, I don't have many useful skills. I didn't really have my life together when things were normal," Ren said, looking away from the old man.

"Not many people at your age have their life sorted out. Heck, some people my age still didn't know what they were doing with themselves. It was okay not to have a plan. Turns out things didn't go to plan anyway, even if you did know what you were doing." Ru started redressing Ren's leg. "We'll find you a purpose. You'll be good at something." Ru looked up at Ren for a minute and smiled, the wrinkles around his eyes deepening with his cheery gaze. Ren smiled back. This man reminded him of his own grandfather. The only paternal figure he'd ever had and he was glad that he was here helping him.

"Everyone seems nice here," Ren said when Ru got back to his job.

"We're a family. There are a few who cause some trouble but Gin keeps everyone in check."

"How long has this clan been about for?" Ren asked.

"We established about a few months after the first drop. Gin and his father—" Shouts from down the hall cut Ru off. He stayed quiet and listened for another moment. It was muffled and far away but the words reached their ears. 'Mutants!'

Ru tied off Ren's bandage and stood, leaving the room as quick as his old bones allowed. Ren panicked. He didn't know what to do. He wanted to help, but he might get in the way. Those creatures terrified him. 'An extra pair of hands is useful regardless.' Ru's words echoed through his head. He growled at himself for even thinking twice about it. "Let's go, Briggs," Ren said.

He stood with care and limped towards the doorway. They made steady progress through the fabric halls. He didn't know where he was going but he followed the sounds of the commotion. He passed the main hall that he'd been dragged into yesterday, it was full of the elderly and the children of the clan. Ren continued onwards. The shouts got louder and now he could hear *them*. The feral, but still human screams. They rounded the last corner and stepped into chaos. People were bleeding in the hallway. Ru crouched over a woman, trying to stop her from bleeding out. Ren pulled his pocket knife out and stepped outside.

It was mayhem. There were at least fifteen mutants, all attacking the clan's fittest members. Ren had never seen this many attacking together. A clansman got brought to the ground in front of Ren; a small infected woman lay on top of him trying to bite his face. Her grey hands pulling at his clothes and arms. Black goo weeping from the holes on his arms and body, falling onto his armour. Ren sprung forwards and kicked it in the side as hard as possible. The force knocked him off balance a little. Briggs jumped over the fallen man and grabbed the mutant by the throat. He thrashed his head, ignoring it as it pulled at his fur. It stopped moving after one last powerful thrash. Briggs dropped its lifeless body. The clansman stood up and handed Ren a bigger blade. "Stick to me," he shouted.

They stood elbow to elbow and advanced on another creature. Ren didn't swing first; he couldn't make himself attack. Its eyes, still too human, looking at him. The clansman however didn't have the same hang ups. He hacked his knife into the side of its neck until it fell dead. He didn't say anything to Ren, just stuck right by his side as they moved into the middle of the scuffle. Briggs growled beside him and he span to look. A mutant was an inch from his face. It screamed at him and lifted its hand to grab him. Briggs yanked its other hand, pulling it to the ground. He yelped when it struck out at him. Ren gasped and kicked it, then before he could think, his blade was in its head.

Blood poured from the wound, matting its patchy hair. He let the hilt go, as it collapsed, the knife staying put. Briggs moved from under it and returned to Ren's side. He put his hands on his head and crouched down. He forced his fists into his eyes, trying desperately to banish that image from his head. He'd gone deaf to what was happening around him, he didn't care. He just wanted that image to go away.

A hand clapped down onto his shoulder, suddenly. He thrashed his arms towards it, falling backwards. It was the man he was sticking by. He stared at the wide-eyed Ren through his long sandy bangs.

"You're okay, kid," he said softly.

It was quiet around them. Ren looked about. The mutants were lying lifeless on the floor and the clan stood tall among the corpses. He looked back up at the man in front of him.

"You're good. They're all downed," he said again, smiling. "Thanks for having my back there. You and your dog really saved me."

He had saved him. He probably could have overpowered that mutant but Ren had stepped in without really thinking. He was still shaking and his throat tight.

"Come on, let me help you up," the clansman said, hauling Ren off the ground and then pulling his arm over his shoulders. Ren's leg started to hurt.

In the thick of it he hadn't even felt it, but now it hurt with every tiny bit of weight he put on it. "I'm Felix," the man said as they wandered back towards the base entrance. "You're Rin, right?"

"Ren."

"Oh yeah, that was it. Nice to meet you properly. You're as bad as the clan are speculating then." Felix grinned.

"I wouldn't say that," Ren said, feeling his cheeks heat up.

"Nah man. You're super cool. I seriously owe you," Felix said.

Felix helped Ren into the main hall. Everyone was forming a circle around the room. He lowered Ren to the ground.

"I'm going to go help the others get inside. You stay here," Felix said before running out the door. Briggs hopped over. Ren took his injured paw into his hand and rubbed his long foreleg.

"Did that hurt you, big guy?" Ren asked. Briggs lay down beside him carefully, resting his chin on Ren's leg. They watched as the clan members were brought in from outside. Most, luckily, were unharmed or had minor scrapes. A couple were holding bloody wounds, but none seemed too urgent. Ru hadn't come in so Ren assumed he was treating the ones with more severe injuries outside. The children left the care of the elders and reunited with their parents. This whole situation seeming so rehearsed and orderly.

Gin entered. He slumped down on his seat looking tired. His hair was falling out of the tie and he pushed the wispy bits out of his face. He closed his eyes and let his head fall back against the rest of his chair. No one was paying attention to him aside from Ren. He'd half expected him to come in and say something but everyone simply sat in silence, relieved that it was over.

Ren could hear something outside the room. The sounds of people arguing were approaching the hall. Everyone inside looked to the door to see what was going on. A small man got pushed into the room. He stumbled forwards before falling onto his stomach. He gripped his wrist and curled onto his side. Gin opened his eyes. A group of much bigger clan members strode in after him.

"He was hiding!" the man at the front shouted, pointing to the boy on the floor. "He was deserting the clan in our time of need!"

The boy tried to speak but he received a kicked to the stomach before he could form the words. Ren jumped at the impact of it. Briggs sat up and pinned his ears down, fixing the group with a stare. Gin stood and crossed the room.

"There's no space here for cowards," the only woman of the three yelled.

"No service, no food! Those are the rules," the first shouted. The boy stammered as Gin started to approach again.

Gin looked menacing now. Ren couldn't tell if it was because he was dishevelled or if he was genuinely angry.

"What happened?" Gin asked, his voice controlled.

"I-I saw them get hurt... hurt and... and I didn't know what to do. I didn't have a weapon. I got injured on the last—" The boy couldn't finish before the first guy kicked him back down.

"He needs to be kicked out!" the brute shouted.

"Leave him alone!" Ren yelled across the room. He stood as swift as his leg would allow and joined the group. Briggs stalked behind him, putting himself between Ren and the aggressive man.

"Stay out of it, wanderer!" the man shouted.

"Axel!" Gin snapped at him.

He ignored him. "You just gonna sit on the floor screaming again, forcing Felix to protect you? People are hyping you up but I think you just got lucky." He spat at Ren's feet.

"Stop!" Gin barked, but he remained a mere audience member. Axel took a single step towards Ren. Briggs barked three times, baring his teeth and fixing his eyes on the man. He growled with his hackles raised, pinning the man in place.

With the same fury as his dog, Ren yelled, "You're spouting about the good of the clan by turning on one of its members! He's injured, even I could see that from over there!" Ren pointed over to where he'd been sitting moments ago. "Guess you're too dumb and pig-headed to see. He's human! Even if he didn't help, because he was scared, he's still only human! You monster!"

Axel swung his fist at Ren but Gin grabbed it before even Briggs could react. His other hand came to rest on Ren's shoulder surprisingly softly, pulling Ren's energy down a level.

"Cut it out!" he ordered to Axel.

"You, are going to hurt yourself." Gin's tone becoming far quieter when he spoke to Ren. He let them both go and knelt in front of the accused.

"Let me see, Finn," he said.

Finn offered him his wrist, pulling his sleeve up. It was black and swollen. Gin sighed. He stood to his full height, before helping Finn up as well.

"You go back to your room and rest. Once Ru is free, get

him to splint that," Gin said to Finn. Finn's bottom lip trembled but he did as he was told, walking quickly from the room.

"You too, Ren. You shouldn't be out of bed anyway."

"I'm fine," Ren dismissed.

"Go." Gin harshened his tone ever so slightly before softening it again. "You and Briggs have done more than enough today, thank you."

Ren decided to do as he was told. It might not be very good for the clan's morale if he started arguing with Gin. He hobbled from the room.

"Brigadier, come," Ren called after Briggs when he stayed to stare at Axel a little longer.

"You're just gonna let him talk to me like that?" He heard Axel say to Gin, but didn't hear the leader's response as he was too far down the hallway.

Chapter 7

"I knew you were going to be trouble when you got here," Ru said as he entered Ren's room the next day. Ren braced himself for an earful. "I heard you shouting at Gin. And that's all he's been able to talk about since. He may be the leader but it doesn't take much to perplex the poor soul."

"Yeah, I'm sor—uh what?" Ren snapped out of his auto response.

"What I'm saying is, he's sensitive. Not that he lets anyone know that. And you, for some reason, keep throwing him through a loop," Ru said, he had his hands on his hip like a mother scolding a child.

That confused Ren. "I'm not exactly sure what I've done," he admitted.

"Doesn't matter," Ru said, getting on with cleaning Ren's wound.

"I'm not doing anything on purpose," Ren said, pushing the subject a little.

"Gin's a strange man. That's all I can really say because I don't fully understand him either sometimes," Ru said.

They fell into a silence. Ren could see that even after a couple of days his injury was healing well, thanks to Ru's care.

"Thank you for yesterday," Ru said suddenly, "It was of great help to us."

"Oh, it's okay." Ren smiled.

"That was a freak attack, I've only seen that happen a

couple times."

"Did lots of people get hurt?"

"Only a couple had serious injuries but providing they don't get infections they should be fine," Ru answered.

"With you looking after them, I'm sure they'll be fine." Ren smiled.

"If you can start wandering about a bit, that'd be good for you. Maybe try coming to the hall for meals," Ru said, ignoring Ren's compliment.

"Okay, I will," Ren said.

"We'll be moving base soon as well; you need to get some strength up because it's a long trip," Ru continued.

"Why?"

"Because you won't make it otherwise?" Ru said a little patronizing.

"No, why do you move bases?" Ren smiled.

"Oh, because that way we can control more land. If we have a consistent presence in two different areas then we can keep control of more regions," Ru explained.

"I see," Ren said.

Ru finished up, they said their good byes and he left again.

"What do you think he meant by that, Briggs?" Ren asked. He still couldn't figure out what Ru had said. Gin didn't seem like the kind of person to get flustered. Nor did Ren really even know what he was getting flustered over. Ren shook his head. He couldn't be bothered to figure that out for now. It probably wasn't a big deal anyway.

***

Ren took Ru's advice. The evening came and Ren was

hobbling around the base; Briggs wandering by his side. He didn't really know where he was going. He'd been out of his room only a handful of times so he was just exploring. Briggs lifted his nose, sniffing the air. He looked to Ren who was watching him, then slowly stalked off down the halls, turning his head to see if Ren was following. Ren did follow.

The dog led him down the halls until Ren could smell what he was smelling. Dinner was being cooked. Briggs had shown him to the kitchen. Ren peaked in through the open hole in the tent walls. It was the only room with metal walls and floor. It had one lady in it, bustling around, stirring pots and chopping on the tables. She looked up as she sensed Ren watching her.

She offered a kind smile and said, "I hear you're the one who saved our Felix." She had a thick South Asian accent. Ren stepped into the room and looked at the floor.

"It was more Briggs," he said, smiling.

"Well, we thank you anyway." She pushed her knife through the piece of meat she was cutting and threw Briggs an offcut. He jumped to catch it, always eager to accept offerings.

"Do you cook for everyone, by yourself?" Ren asked.

"Yes! I love cooking so it's no sweat off my back. I missed it before I lived with this clan." Her tone then softened and sounded almost sad. "I was so used to cooking for a large family."

Ren smiled sadly to her.

She grinned wide. "So, it reminds me of home to cook for this lot! I like doing my part." Her voice lifted again. "It'll be done soon, head to the hall with everyone else."

"Yes, I will." Ren turned away from the woman cooking, "Um… where is it?" he said, turning back suddenly,

47

remembering he didn't actually know.

"Down the hall on the left." She smiled at him.

"Thanks." Ren returned her smile.

They left. Ren followed the cook's instruction and started down the hall.

"You bothering Nadi now?" a voice called from behind him. Ren turned to see Gin strolling towards them. He bent to pet Briggs's head when he reached the pair.

"No!" Ren said playfully defensive. "Was just checking she didn't need help, slaving away for you lot."

Gin smirked. "She doesn't mind and we appreciate her greatly."

"Yeah, she said."

"It's good to see you up," Gin said, his hand coming up to play with the leather strap on his shoulder.

"Ru said I should. It's hurting less now," he said.

"Good. That's good," Gin said.

They stood in silence for a moment. Neither of them knowing what to say. "We should probably get to the hall," Ren said.

"Yes, Nadi doesn't mess around with late comers." Gin smiled, leading the way to the main hall. "But, if she's running late, I'm blaming you for bugging her."

"No, that's not fair!" Ren frowned at him.

"It's one hundred per cent fair," Gin teased. "In fact, I might just give your share to Briggs."

"He certainly wouldn't complain about that. He'll sell anyone out for an extra dinner." Briggs's ears pricked forwards when he said 'dinner'.

"I think anyone would in this place." Gin laughed.

They entered the main hall. It was buzzing with people.

The warm glow of the torches bathed everyone in a soft orange light. It felt warm and homely.

"Do you want to sit with me?" Gin asked quietly.

Ren answered quickly, trying not to let on how off guard that caught him, "Yeah okay." Gin nodded to him and silently led him across the hall.

People gathered in a rough circle, everyone seeming to have a place to sit; leaving gaps for people who weren't there yet. They approached a small group of people towards the back. Ren recognised Felix. The two others were squabbling rather loudly.

"I will bet you half my dinner, that you won't find more resources than me next mission!" a tall brown-haired woman said. She was pointing her finger towards a shorter, heavier set man.

"No, no, no," the man said, wagging his finger back at her, "you get distracted too easily."

Gin sat beside Felix; Ren followed suit.

"What are they arguing for now?" Gin asked Felix quietly.

"Gus was bragging about the stuff he found last expedition and Tally said it was a fluke and that overall, she'd found way better stuff. Then they started betting on who could find better stuff next time," Felix summarised in one exhausted breath. Both of them turned to Felix now.

"I wasn't bragging," Gus said.

"And *I* have found better stuff than him!" Tally said.

"Jeez." Gin sighed.

Luckily, dinner was brought into the hall and both of them ceased their bickering. Bowls were passed around the people, no one starting until everyone had something to eat. Ru had joined them now as well. "The Raider activity has increased in the city, Gin," Gus said seriously now.

"We might need to move the clan sooner."

"Do you think they're just passing by or if they're up to something?" Felix asked.

"Don't know."

"They looked like they were searching for something," Ren spoke up. "They were looking through the buildings when we were hiding there. If they're still over there maybe they haven't found it yet?"

"We've rinsed that city dry, there isn't a building we haven't looked through," Gus explained.

"Maybe a place for a new base. If they're going to try and attack, they'd want a base nearby," Tally said.

"We should move the clan, Gin," Ru said.

"Yeah, we'll start packing tomorrow, aim to leave the next day. Keep some scouting routes this way so we don't lose this one." Gin decided.

The group nodded around them, trusting their leader completely.

Chapter 8

Ren helped out where he could the next day. Anyone that needed an extra hand, he helped. That was until Ru had caught him and told him to go to bed and rest up. He didn't want to, but he also didn't want to argue with Ru. After all, he didn't actually know how far they were going to be travelling the next day.

After one more night's rest, and breakfast the next morning, the clan gathered outside the front of the base ready to leave. Everyone was carrying a bag or pulling a small wooden cart. Gin appeared in the entrance of the base, having looked around it one last time. He nodded to Ru, who stood at the front, letting him know they were good to go. Ru and the older members of the clan led the way, setting the pace. The sick and injured followed, being pulled in larger carts by two of the fitter members. Everyone else was between them and Gin, who took his place at the very back.

Ren watched them pass for a moment. "You okay?" Gin asked.

"Yeah, I'm fine. This all just seems so rehearsed," Ren admitted, walking at the back beside Gin.

"We do this about four times a year," Gin explained.

"Really?"

"Yeah, keeps everyone safe and familiar with the area we control."

"You been doing this for a while then?" Ren asked.

"Since the beginning. I was left with my dad and we found a small group, Ru being one of them. We decided the best way to survive would be to bunker down and defend ourselves. And as we got bigger and stronger, we expanded."

"Damn," Ren said, "what happened to your dad, if you don't mind me asking?"

Gin didn't answer straight away, Ren stayed looking forwards giving him time to find the words.

"I didn't notice before he turned. I didn't know what I was looking for, not that there's a cure or anything. Turns out not everyone mutates at the same rate. He'd come from one of the infected zones to get me, the day it all happened. So, it was already too late then but he survived another four months before his eyes and tongue started turning black, then another two before... you know."

"I'm sorry, that's awful." Ren didn't know what to say.

"It's fine, it's been a long time, almost two years now, hasn't it?"

"Two years, really?" Ren's eyebrows raised.

"Yeah, we only know because Ru keeps track. He could probably tell you what the exact date is." Gin smiled. "What about you, where were you when it all went to hell?"

"My grandparent's house. We stayed there a lot because my mum worked in the city that got hit first. Nan and Grandad were out for the day, me and my sister got hit by the shockwave and passed out. Briggs woke me up, frantic," Ren explained.

"How long ago was she taken?"

"Don't know exactly, but it's been a while. Probably a few months now." Ren's jaw clenched tight.

"Yeah, that's probably about right if you came that far on foot," Gin mused.

"Like, I want to believe she's okay still, but I don't…" Ren cut himself off. The denial still preventing him from thinking about that possibility.

"Well, you'll be happy to know that this base we're going to is much closer to the Raider's main base. Or at least we think it's their—" Ren cut him off.

"Where?" he asked.

"I'm not telling you." Gin smirked a little.

"Why?"

Gin's smile fell when Ren looked genuinely heart broken. "Because you'll go off by yourself," he said.

They had stopped walking, without either of them noticing. Ren stared up at him, his brow pulling up in the centre and his lips dragged down. He inhaled sharply and turned his head away from Gin. Gin lowered his head to try and catch Ren's gaze again. He gently placed a hand on Ren's arm and pulled him to keep walking. When Ren fell into step beside him, Gin's hand moved to the small of his back. Gin tensed for a moment when Ren lent against him.

"You'll help me still, won't you?" Ren said, his voice was tiny and weak. He sounded broken and it lit a fire inside Gin again.

"I'll drag their leader to you with my bare hands if I need to."

Ren didn't say anything. He didn't really need to. Because he somehow knew that Gin would do that for him, even if he never asked him to.

***

Night was falling and Ren's leg had just started to ache when the new base rose on the horizon. It stood in the middle of nowhere; nothing around it but a small triangle rock formation to the right of it.

"Almost there now," Gin said, seeing the limp forming in Ren's step. He'd kept an eye on him the whole way, even offered to carry him, or at least his bags at one point. Ren had refused, telling him he was fine rather than admitting that the suggestion had made a shiver run up his spine.

No one wasted any time when they reached the base. They got on with their respective jobs and duties to get the base up and running.

"I'll show you to your room so you can rest up," Gin said, leading Ren inside. Gin carried a burning torch and lit the torches in the hallways they walked down. He took them to a dead end and a cloth door. There were five doorways in total.

"You can have this one," Gin said, "for as long as you need."

"Thanks," Ren said going inside. Gin followed and lit the candles in the room.

"My room's the very end one," Gin said, pointing in the direction of the end of the hall, "if you need anything, ever."

"Thank you," Ren said again.

"I'll come get you when dinner's ready. Probably be later than usual." Gin lingered by the doorway for a minute before he left.

"Weirdo," Ren said, under his breath. He smiled at himself and sat on his bed, rubbing his hands over his eyes.

Briggs's wet nose touched the back of his hand. Ren stroked his dog's head.

"Maybe I'm the weirdo." He laughed at himself. "Whichever it is, I'm ninety per cent sure it's Ru's fault."

He fell back onto his bed, his back and leg thanking him for the rest, finally. Briggs jumped on and laid next to him. He pulled him close and cuddled into his fur. Ren closed his eyes hoping to rest a little before dinner.

***

Ren found this new base much easier to navigate. It was built like a spider's web. The main hall was dead centre and branching hallways connected three larger rings. If Ren got lost, he could just keep walking round until he reached where he needed to be. And as the days passed, he'd begun to learn its layout.

Ren was lent against the doorway of the base, watching Briggs mooch around outside. A group approaching him caught his attention. It was Gin, Tally, Gus and Felix coming down the hall towards him. They had bags on their backs and weapons sheathed on their bodies.

"Where are you lot going?" Ren asked.

"Scavenging." Tally grinned.

"Yeah, you want ta come?" Gus asked.

"I don't think—" Gin started, but Ren interrupted him.

"Sure!" he said, happy for the chance to actually get out for once.

"Ren, isn't your leg sore still?" Gin asked.

"Not really," Ren said, stamping his foot on the ground a couple times.

"We're going to be gone all day," Gin said.

"That's fine." Ren shrugged. "Let me just grab my bag." He turned away to get his stuff.

The group was waiting for him out the front, Ren half

expecting Gin to have convinced them to leave without him. Tally was sat on the floor scratching Briggs's belly. He stood up when he saw Ren come back, shaking all the dirt and sand off.

"You ready?" Gus smiled at him.

Ren nodded and they left the base, crossing the wasteland until a city emerged on the horizon. But they didn't stop inside. Instead, they followed an old road until they reached what would have been a smaller village. These houses were more intact, only showing signs of lack of care and being exposed to the elements. They passed a corner shop. Tally and Felix looked around inside, while the other three continued down the roads.

"We found this place before we moved bases last time, but didn't have time to look around properly," Gus explained to Ren.

"This is the most intact I've seen a village. All the ones I passed through were completely flattened," Ren said, looking around in awe.

"They dropped the bombs down the centre of the country," Gus started. "So, the further away from where the shockwave would have been originally, the more intact everything is."

"Places like this and beyond would be liveable if it wasn't for the freak weather we have now," Gin added.

"And the mutants eating people!" Tally made Ren jump, her and Felix having caught back up to them.

"Yes, and that, Tally." Gin smiled at her.

"Woah, look at that!" Tally yelled, pointing ahead of them.

At the end of the road a gated driveway stretched out in front of them. The tall manor house loomed; half collapsed.

"Bagsy, looking round that," Gin said, quickly.

"Ah, dammit!" Tally said, "I'll come with!"

"Nah, I'll stick with Ren. You guys go look for supplies," Gin ordered.

"*You guys go look for supplies,*" Tally badly impersonated Gin's voice making Ren laugh. She ran off down a branching road before Gin could punish her for it. Gus rolled his eyes, and Felix shook his head, following after her.

"Oh, she's horrid," Gin said, without meaning a single word of it.

They reached the tall metal fence that surrounded the manor house. Gin tried the gate, rattling the padlock that secured a chain around its bars.

"Over there," Ren said, seeing a hole in the bars down the fence from where they were.

Gin stopped Ren when he tried to step through first. Ren shot him a funny look but decided to ignore it. Their footsteps crunched loud on the stony driveway. One side of the manor had completely fallen down, but the other side with the high brick chimney seemed okay. One of the doors was hanging off its hinges, the other completely gone. They looked through the gap together, a long through breeze passed them. Again, Gin stepped in first. A tunnel of darkness stretched out in front of them, light shining through from the back of the house. Gin walked across the marble floor and into a room on the broken down side of the house. Briggs following him out there.

A big wooden staircase ascended off to the side of Ren. He decided to take a look up them. He climbed them carefully, making sure none of the steps were actually broken before he put his full weight on them. The top landing was big and open, the left side leading to two rooms and the other side falling off in broken pieces. Ren looked into the rooms on the left. Only the furniture that wouldn't have fit through the doorway was left. Ren assumed the people who had once lived here had evacuated long before their house started falling down. The creaking of the floorboards sent unpleasant chills up his spine so he turned around to go back down. He heard a shout suddenly.

"REN!" Gin called.

Ren ran across the landing and back down the stairs, his leg collapsing on him just as he reached the bottom two. He fell forwards and skidded along the marble floor a small way. He turned over onto his side when he saw something move in the corner of his eye.

"Ren! Are you okay?" Gin asked, crouching to take a closer look at him. Ren let out a sigh seeing Gin's face but his heart still pounded.

"I'm fine," he said.

"What were you doing? I turned around and you weren't there!" Gin sounded a little frantic.

"I was just looking around upstairs."

"Why? This building is falling to pieces, why would you go upstairs?" Gin asked him, a scowl forming on his lips.

Ren matched his frown. "In case, there was something up there."

"You could have broken your legs falling through the floor."

"Gin, chill out! You've been weird since we split off from the others!" Ren shouted back at him.

"It's because you're being careless." Gin didn't shout. "You're waltzing around the place like there's no danger."

"Stop!" Ren snapped making both Gin and Briggs jump.

"Stop acting like I don't know! I've been wandering around places like this by myself for just as long as you, believe it or not. And I've managed to take care of myself. Why do you insist on babysitting me?"

"Because I worry about you more than anyone else in the clan!" Gin shocked both of them into silence. He looked away as he searched for better words.

"Because you think I'm weak?" Ren's voice was small, actually a little hurt by that.

"No!" Gin looked back at him, concern on his face. "Because you're strong and you spend all your time helping other people. I'm not convinced you even care about how you, yourself, are doing."

Ren finally looked away from him. His brow frowned and his lips pinched together.

"Are you okay?" Gin asked him.

"Yeah, my leg is just—" he started but Gin interrupted him.

"No, are you actually all right?" Gin said, lifting Ren's chin to make him look him in the eyes.

"No," Ren admitted, "I'm tired."

Gin's hand slid to cup his cheek and Ren took hold of his wrist, pressing into the touch. Gin gently pulled Ren forwards. Ren took the invitation to take hold of Gin, pulling their bodies together. Gin's strong arms squeezed him, his chin resting on Gin's shoulder.

"I didn't mean what I said earlier," Gin whispered.

"No, I was being careless. Because you're right, I don't care what happens to me," Ren said.

"Good thing then, that I'm here to watch your back now." Gin smiled against the side of his head. Ren pulled away.

"Is that why you didn't want me to come?" he asked.

"Was I being that obvious?" Gin fiddled with the buckle on his chest plate with one hand. Ren nodded at him, raising his eyebrows and pushing his lips together.

"Well, I am genuinely worried about your leg. But yes, I wanted you to stay because I know you'll be safe back at the base and not falling down flights of stairs," Gin teased.

"It's your fault for screaming bloody murder."

"I'll just let you get left behind next time, that's fine," Gin said standing up.

He started walking away with his arms crossed and his nose petulantly in the air. When Ren didn't follow, he turned and looked at him seriously.

"I think I might have actually hurt myself a bit," Ren admitted, still sat on the floor. Gin was back at his side in a second, helping him off the floor with care.

"I think I twisted my knee or something. I think it'll walk off," Ren said.

"I can carry you back," Gin offered.

"No thanks, wouldn't want you to put your back out, old man." Ren grinned.

"Ol-Old man? There isn't that many years between us!" Gin gasped.

"Yeah, you must be old, if you think I need babysitting so bad."

"Fine then, but Ru must be a walking corpse at this point then." Gin laughed, leaving the building.

Ren laughed too. "How cruel! I'm going to tell him that when we get back."

"And I'll tell him you started it."

"Babies are allowed to start it."

They continued squabbling until they met up with the others again. They'd found a good number of supplies and they were ready to head back. Ren couldn't wait to get some food and go to bed; the emotions and long journey having drained him completely. But his heart, for once, felt lighter than ever.

***

Briggs woke Ren up in the middle of the night. Ren was groggy and it took him a minute to wake up properly. With a full belly after dinner, it hadn't taken him long to go back to sleep. Briggs whined at him again. Ren pulled some trousers, his trainers and a hoodie over his bare skin. Briggs waited for him at the door.

"Yeah, I'm coming," Ren whispered.

They walked down the dark halls together. In his tired state, Ren didn't exactly know where he was going so, he let Briggs lead the way. His claws and Ren's footsteps were the only noises around them. The material of the door was flapping in the wind. Ren stood just inside as Briggs left. He'd been out there a while so Ren looked to find him. He was sniffing at the floor right in front of the entrance.

"Get in, man," Ren whispered harshly. He looked up at Ren for a moment but then turned and walked away, his head to the floor again. Ren frowned at his strange behaviour.

Ren stepped out of the base and walked up to Briggs. He looked at where he was sniffing. Footprints headed away from the base. He looked back towards the base; his own set of footprints stood next to a fainter set. They walked further away from the base. Ren followed them, squinting into the darkness. A sick feeling filled his stomach. He had an idea who they could belong to but hoped he was terribly wrong.

Against his better judgement he followed the footprints. They were leading towards the rock formation by the base. Ren picked up the pace. Briggs loped alongside of him and he mentally thanked Ru for healing his dog's leg.

The shadows of the rocks grew suddenly, the blue flash brightening the wasteland for a moment. Ren skidded to a stop and watched as a person was thrown out from behind the rocks. He landed hard against the dirt. Tears welled in Ren's eyes as he ran to his aid. He fell to his knees beside Gin. His eyes were closed and his chest rose and fell slowly. Gin had a lightning strike up his chest. The Blue Bolt had caught him just above his navel and it ripped a fork up and across his chest. It branched across, covering his whole chest in bleeding wounds. The remains of his shirt were burnt and torn.

Briggs's growl distracted him. He looked to him and followed his line of sight. Like hyenas, they stalked around the sides of the rock. Four Raiders approached, grins on their faces.

"Look! Two of his dogs have come to save him," one of them cackled, pointing his knife towards him. Ren scowled at him. He looked back to Gin; his eyes were open now. Weakly, he lifted his hand to grab Ren's arm.

"You have to go." He was barely able to speak. "They followed us…from the other base… they're going to attack… you need to… get the clan to leave," he spoke between long shallow breaths. He wanted to protect his clan. But Ren needed to protect him.

"I can't, Gin," Ren said, "I'm not leaving you here to die a useless death." He stood ignoring Gin's commands and pleas. Ren stood alongside Briggs. The dog had his head low and his hackles raised high off his back. Gin coughed his name, begging for him not to do this.

"You really want to fight us?" a Raider called. "You should listen to your leader."

"You deserve to rot!" Ren shouted back. He felt around his back pocket. A tiny amount of relief washed over him when his fingers grazed his pocket knife. He unfolded the blade and held it up defensively.

"Fine, but we'll kill you first," another shouted.

All four Raiders advanced on Ren and Briggs. Ren's heart jumped in his throat. His mind raced, trying to find a way out. But there wasn't anything he could do, not with himself and Gin getting out alive. Ren swallowed thickly. *Fine then. Time to repay the Opal Foxes for looking after me. I'm sorry Flo, you might need to wait a little longer for me to come get you.*

The Raiders ran towards him. Ren grabbed Briggs stopping him from attacking first. When the first man reached him, Ren dodged his swing. The second came out of nowhere, striking him in the face. It knocked him off balance, Ren tripped and fell to the floor. He braced himself for the beating, but it didn't come. Briggs had jumped over him and was pushing the two Raiders back. As one swung for him, he grabbed her wrist, pulling her to the ground snapping the bone in his jaw. She screamed out and her comrade kicked Briggs in the flank. He yelped but continued to thrash the woman's broken arm. The male Raider lent down to grab him; a mistake. Briggs let go of the Raider's arm and sunk his teeth into the man's face.

The scream caused the other two Raiders to advance now. Ren pushed himself off the floor when they approached with caution. One swung his blade at him, Ren jumped away as the blade came level with his face. A long slash of blood rose on his cheek. Ren needed to land a hit.

Frustrated by Ren's ability to avoid getting hit, the final Raider took his turn. His strikes were hard and disorienting. Ren stayed on his feet but couldn't get his own hit in.

Briggs's squeal distracted him for a single moment. The last Raider he was fighting had picked him up and thrown him across the wasteland. He had fistfuls of his fur in his hands. A fist collided with Ren's face, then a foot followed to his stomach. The wind was thrown out of his lungs and once again his knees hit the floor. The Raider climbed on top of him and repeatedly punched his knuckles into Ren's face.

Through his swelling eyes Ren saw Briggs's limp body. Then he looked to Gin, he was still trying to push himself off the ground to help. Tears blurred his vision then the edges of his eyesight blackened. The last thing he could hear before his vision went completely black was Gin, shouting his name.

Chapter 9

Ren's head was spinning when he finally woke up again. It was so dark; he could barely see. He felt like he would throw up. His hands lifted to his face and he winced when he touched the swollen flesh. He was sure his nose was broken. He tasted blood when he licked his lip; it was numb and tingling. But other than his face, he didn't think there was any more major damage.

Ren looked around himself now. He seemed to be in some sort of cage, tall metal bars rose from the ground and closed above him. A metal candle stick stood outside of his cell; it gave off minimal light. To his right another cell, inside Gin lay on the floor.

Ren's heart pumped harder. A different kind of sickness washed over him as he forced his limbs to work. Ren crawled across the floor to reach Gin. The sound of his own breathing filled his ears. He reached through the bars and grabbed Gin's arm, pulling him across the dirt floor. He pressed his first and middle finger against Gin's neck. His hands shook when he couldn't feel anything. Tears swelled in his eyes. He pushed harder, moving his fingers a little.

There!

Gin's pulse pressed against the tips of his fingers. Ren scrubbed his hands over his eyes trying to clear his eyesight. Ren lent against the bars as his breath caught. He sobbed into his knees. His mind was racing, but with no real thoughts or feelings, just a mess of incoherent panic. Ren jerked his head up when he heard a groan next to him.

Gin's eyes were squinting up at him. He stared at Ren's stricken face. His hand weakly lifted and shakily slipped in between the bars, his knuckles touching Ren's arm. Ren grabbed his hand and held the back of it to his face. It was cold against his cheek, but his fingers slowly curled around Ren's own.

"Sorry," Gin whispered; his voice gravelly.

"You're dumb," Ren said, a new wave of tears falling.

"Hmm," Gin hummed back. He closed his eyes again.

Ren looked at Gin's chest. A thin bandage covered it. Clearly, they didn't want them dead or they would let Gin just bleed out.

"You should have left me," Gin said, his eyes still closed.

"No!" Ren snapped, "I shouldn't have. Plus, Briggs wouldn't have just walked—" Ren stopped, a sharp gasp leaving his throat. He looked around the empty room.

"Briggs isn't here," Ren said weakly.

"They probably left him there. He would have gone back to the base." Gin tried to comfort him.

"I hope so," Ren said, settling back against the bars. "He's too old to be dealing with stuff like this."

"Sorry," Gin said again.

"Stop saying that."

Silence settled between them. Gin's hand shook gently in Ren's. "Is it sore?" Ren asked him.

"A little, aches when I breathe," Gin answered him.

Ren didn't know what to say because there wasn't anything he could do.

Voices from outside the room interrupted them. The

room's material door lifted and two men and a woman walked in. The men were much like the Raiders he'd seen before, both shirtless with the red lines and shapes painted on them. They had big blades sheathed in various places on their bodies. The woman came to stand in the middle, just in front of their cells.

She was wearing a metal chest plate with the red patterns on. A leather belt secured her animal skin leggings to her body. She had sturdy combat boots on, one of which had grey tape wrapped around the toe. The right side of her head was shaved, the rest of her hair – the ends bleach blonde, and the rest her natural colour – was plaited and laying over her shoulder. Her face twisted into a malicious smirk and evil lit her eyes ablaze.

She came and crouched down behind the bars. Ren scowled at her when their gaze met. He noticed a circle of gold hanging around her neck. The Raider's emblem had been crudely scratched into it; a skull with crosses for eyes and a dagger in its head.

She smirked at Ren and then looked to Gin. He'd pushed himself up off the floor to meet her eye.

"Oh, how the mighty have fallen." She sighed. "How does it feel being the one on the bottom, Fox leader?"

"What do you want?" Gin said, not playing her game.

"What I want? You seem to forget that you started this. Don't feel bad now you've finally lost."

"You were sending scouts near my clan and you expect me not to do anything."

"Oh, did I? I hadn't noticed." She laughed at Gin's rising anger. "You did make life easier when you moved closer to us. You fell right into my hands. I've been trying for so long to overthrow you and here we are." She grinned.

Ren looked between them, neither of them dropped the

others gaze. Even though Gin was in incredible pain he still stood powerful against this rogue force.

"However," the Raider leader started, "we're not completely evil. I've got the perfect trial for you. If you can beat it, I'll let you go free. And your little... friend here."

"What kind of trial?" Gin asked.

"We'll put you up against one of our pets and we'll see who wins. If you win, you get your freedom, if you lose... well you lose," she explained.

"Like a fight?" Ren asked shakily.

"Yes, a fight." She grinned at him.

"How can I trust you will actually let us go?" Gin asked.

"Now, now. I may be crooked but I still have honour." She offered her hand like a snake through the bars.

"Deal." Gin grabbed her hand and yanked her forwards, holding her in a vice grip. "You turn back on that and I'll have your head," he growled at her.

"You stay in your territory and I'll stay in mine. It'll be good for me to get you out of my hair." Gin let her go and she stood up.

"One last thing," Gin said, "the dog that was on the wasteland with us. Where is it?"

"Oh, the one that disfigured one of my best men? They left it there to die," she cackled when Ren's face dropped in horror. "Sweet dreams!"

Then they were gone, leaving Ren and Gin with the devastating news.

Silence stretched between them. Ren unable to process what he'd just been told and Gin not sure what to say. Gin watched him stare straight ahead at the place the Raider leader had been standing. His breathing was shaking his whole body.

Then his face suddenly screwed up.

He turned to Gin, "Why are you so stupid?" he shouted. "Do you have a death wish? Is living really that hard for you?"

Gin stared at him wide-eyed as tears began to fall from Ren's eyes.

"You're sick! I hate you! There could have been another way!" Ren cried. "What would Ru think of you just throwing your life away like that?"

"There isn't another way though, Ren," Gin said.

"We could escape!"

"And go where? If we get out, which is highly unlikely because there will be Raiders literally everywhere, then what? Go and die in the heat of the wasteland or in a sandstorm?" Gin said frankly, but his tone was soft.

"You'll die," Ren sobbed; his anger now subsided into sorrow.

"I'll try my best not to."

"You're not going to be able to fight, you're hurt. Like you said when we first met. No one survives a Blue Bolt wound."

"You're still alive." Gin smiled weakly.

"It's hardly the same."

"I know." Gin lent against the bars and grabbed Ren. Ren willingly scooted closer. He rested his head next to Gin's, they didn't touch; the bars a reminder of their hopeless situation.

"I'm going to have to cut my hair off." Gin broke the silence.

"What?" Ren looked over to him.

A grin spread across Gin's lips. "Gus once tried to persuade me to shave my head like him. I said I liked it long so we made a bet. It was not long after I had a nasty encounter with a mutant, so he said, next time I almost die I have to shave my hair off. So, I've been growing it out of spite basically ever since."

Ren surprised himself when he laughed. "You two are so dumb."

"Yeah maybe." Gin smiled. "But it's kept me out of trouble."

"Clearly not any more though."

"I'm sorry."

"Stop," Ren said.

"No, I am. This is all my fault. Briggs would be okay if I hadn't—"

"Stop! I said, stop!" Hearing his name made Ren's heart ache again. "He was too old. I was lucky he made it this far."

Gin took Ren's hand. Ren squeezed it. Gin lifted Ren's hand to his lips, holding it there for a minute, before lowering it again between them.

"The clan would have found him and they would have dealt with him respectfully," Gin said.

"I hope so."

"They all loved him. Both of you, if I'm honest. You were a very refreshing presence… especially for me." Gin trailed off at the end of his sentence.

"I think I finally get what Ru meant now."

"That snitch! What's he been saying?" Gin teased.

"Just that you're sensitive." Ren smiled.

Gin shook his head. "Can't trust nobody with nothing."

"I mean it has been painfully obvious since he pointed it out."

They settled again into a sorrow-filled silence. No amount of joking about could change the inevitable. Ren didn't want to lose anyone else. He didn't want to make it out alive if he was going to be alone again. He wanted to find his sister, but the thought of losing Gin now was painful. He suddenly hated himself for being so selfish. He'd dragged Briggs along with him instead of putting him out of his misery in the beginning; this wasn't a world for a dog to live in. He was sorry for making Gin worry about him so much, but he was scared of being alone.

"I don't hate you," Ren whispered.

"I know." Gin smiled at him. It was a hurting, sad smile. Because they both knew. Gin was putting on a brave face but Ren could see the tension in his jaw.

Voices came from outside their room. Ren's heart thumped harder in his chest. Gin squeezed his hand tighter. Ren's vision blurred with tears.

"I'll come back," Gin said looking Ren square in the eyes. "I'll come back and we'll go back to the base together." Gin's hands lifted to hold each side of Ren's face. They trembled a little against the side of his head. Ren did the same, tangling his fingers into Gin's hair. Gin wiped the tears away with his thumb. "We'll go home together. And we'll have dinner with everyone and go to bed, because I'm tired and I'm going to sleep for a whole month anyway."

Ren sobbed a laugh. "We'll go to bed together?" he asked.

"Yeah, because when I survive this, I'm never going to let you be alone again."

The Raiders entered the room. Ren flinched; gripping Gin tighter. He squeezed his eyes shut for a second. Gin's hand left Ren's face and gripped his wrists. He pulled Ren's hands from his face.

"I'll come back," he said, pushing Ren's hands back

towards himself. Ren shook his head, silently pleading for Gin not to do this.

"Please, Gin," Ren begged. Gin let him go as the Raiders entered his cell.

"Gin, please!" Ren reached through the bars. His fingers brushed against Gin's shirt but the Raiders pulled him away and out of Ren's grip.

"Please don't take him," Ren cried, "GIN! Please!" His voice cracked.

Gin's steps were shaky as he was led from the cell, he was hunched over a little and one of his hands held his side. The Raiders led him towards the door, he turned his head one last time.

"I will come back for you," Gin said, his final words before he disappeared behind the fabric door.

"NO!" Ren protested, repeating it at the top of his lungs. He cried helplessly on the floor of his cell. He cried out, hitting his fists against the floor, but it was all useless; nothing was going to bring him back. He was alone again. And completely useless to Gin.

Chapter 10

Ren's cries subsided into frustration. He sat up and pushed the balls of his palms into his eyes. He stayed like that until his breathing calmed and he could think straight again. Crying on the floor wasn't going to help Gin; sitting around in this cell wasn't going to help him either. He stood up – his leg shaky and unsteady – to investigate the door to the cell. There was a thick chain looped twice around the door and its frame, secured with a heavy padlock. Ren jiggled the padlock and pulled at the door. It rattled and moved an inch, but didn't provide an escape. Ren looked around the room outside his cell. The Raiders weren't dumb enough to just leave the keys hanging up somewhere in the room, but they could be on a person dumb enough to come into the room, Ren thought.

Ren looked around himself. The only moveable object in the room was the torch stand just outside his cell. It was rickety, made up of two metal pipes tied together with string. It slanted a little to the left, the base barely keeping all three feet on the ground. Ren lent through the bars, pushing himself against the metal to extend his reach as much as possible. His fingers just grasped the metal. He flinched when it scraped along the floor. He was still, listening if the noise had alerted anyone. No one came. He grabbed it properly and lifted it closer to his cell.

His fingers were cold and slow as he tried to untie the knots holding the torch stand together. They were tight and the string was too thick to snap. His hands were shaking as his only option started to seem impossible. The torch wobbled and then suddenly fell, taking the top pole with it. It clattered to the floor making a loud noise and plunging the room into darkness.

A shout came from outside and Ren hid in the corner, this was his chance. The door opened briefly filling the room with light.

"What the hell are you doing in here?" the guard grumbled. As he stepped into the room, he plunged them back into darkness.

He growled in his throat, "I'm missing all the fun, finally that Fox bastard is going to be ripped to shreds and I'm here babysitting his rent boy." His steps crossed the room and he fumbled with the chain on the door. "Where are ya?" he called.

Ren's eyes had adjusted to the dark. He heard the chain slide from around the bars and the door swing open. Ren's heart pounded as the Raider guard stepped into his cell. But the anger in his veins tightened his grip on the pipe and he swung. It collided with the man's face, he shouted and fell back to the floor. Ren raised the bar over his head and swung it down again and again, until the Raider went quiet. Ren felt over the man's body. He found the keys and a lighter. Ren flipped open the lid, flicked the wheel and quickly jumped back away from the Raider.

Ren stared, rooted to the spot by the sight. The bloodied bar lay next to the Raider; his beaten, lifeless face staring up at the ceiling. Ren's head swayed. He stepped away from the body, until his back hit the wall of the cell. He looked down; his clothes covered with red splatters. He dropped the lighter and his stomach twisted sharply; he threw up. He coughed and heaved, his mind forcing him to see the Raider that he'd killed without mercy.

Ren swallowed thickly, closing his eyes for a minute. He had to move on, he had to help Gin. Ren grabbed the lighter and lit it again. He stared straight ahead, refusing to look at the Raider again. Carefully, he stood, holding onto the bars to steady himself. He walked out of his cell and left the room not looking back at what he'd done.

***

Unlike the Fox base, this base had no rhyme or reason. This base twisted and turned so much that Ren got lost very quickly. It was empty and quiet. Only a whistle of noise called down the halls to him. He followed the noise. They were shouts, cheers in fact.

Ren's stomach twisted, the floor seeming to sway under his steps. He was too late. Ren scowled at himself, until he laid eyes on Gin again, he wasn't too late. The shouts turned into words. "GET HIM!" And cries of joy reached Ren's ears. He picked up the pace, rounding a corner. In the right side of the wall there was an opening.

It was bright and led out into a massive stadium. The first layer of seats full with Raiders, sat a couple feet above Ren's head. It climbed up higher and higher, the top level dizzily high above his head. A mighty crash dragged Ren's attention forwards. There was a tall, wooden fence in front of him. He stepped towards it, glancing over his shoulder to see if anyone was watching him. There was a small gap in the fencing that he could look through.

He hated himself when a wave of relief washed over him

upon seeing that the man in the arena was not Gin. A terrified young man ran around the dusty arena. He begged and pleaded for mercy, for anyone to help him but was only met with laughter. Ren focused on the monster that was chasing him. She was the least altered he'd ever seen a mutant. She was small and thin; she had a dirty dress covering her greying body; her hair matted and patchy; one of her legs was twice the size of the other, the radiation swelling the flesh. It caused her to limp slowly towards her prey. She had the same oozing holes on her body as they all did. She followed the man without much zealous. Now and then running to catch up with him before running out of energy again. The man turned, waving his small knife at the mutant. He was hysterical, trying to ward off his assailant. He tripped over his own feet and fell on his back. This sparked the mutant's attention. She growled and lunged forwards, closing the gap and jumping onto the man. Ren turned away as she lifted her head, mouth open wide. But he could still see an image of the young man's life ending in his imagination. The crowd roared.

"Oh, bad luck!" a male's voice spoke above the cheers of the crowd. "While the arena is cleared let's make some noise for our next contestant. Now this one is very special and many of you might know him." This caught Ren's attention. "We've finally caught him, viewers." The crowd started to shout and cheer. "The Opal Fox Leader, everyone!" The Raiders erupted once again. Ren looked into the arena, trying to get a sight of Gin.

A pair of wooden gates opened at the far end of the arena. Gin walked out, armed only with a single short blade. He looked horrid. Even though he hadn't been gone from Ren's side for long, he looked so tired. They'd definitely roughed him up a bit while he was waiting for his turn. Gin stopped and looked straight ahead. Ren followed his gaze. The Raider leader, sat sprawled across a plush throne high in the arena, met Gin's gaze. Ren could see the smug smirk on her face, even from where he was stood.

"Now, for our special contestant, we have a very special opponent." The voice shouted over the arena again, "Our reigning champion who hasn't lost a fight yet, obviously or he'd be dead." The man laughed maniacally. "The one, the only, TITAN!"

Another set of doors across from Gin opened. The air was stolen from Ren's lungs when he looked at the beast that stepped out.

It stood at least a foot taller than Gin and twice his width easily. Massive deformed muscles bulged under its poorly fitting clothing. Its skin was a grey tone like most of the other mutants. It growled to itself, foaming from the mouth. It clocked Gin in the middle of the arena and let out a deafening roar. Gin didn't flinch. He held the small blade in front of himself and the mutant charged at him.

Gin kited it around the arena; Ren could see that he was just trying to buy time. It got close, swiping its fist at Gin. Gin forced his knife into its forearm. The monster growled, lifting Gin clean off the ground as he tried to keep hold of his weapon. The blade released from Titan's flesh as he threw Gin to the side.

The crowd whooping and cheering. Ren gasped out his name when Gin landed close to the gap he was peeking through. Gin pulled himself onto his knees and forearms. His head flew up at the sound of Ren's voice.

Wide-eyed, they stared at each other and Gin smiled at

him. He was tired, beads of sweat falling down his forehead, but he smiled. The creature continued to approach and Gin pulled his eyes away from Ren to run into open space again. Ren didn't want to leave; he didn't want Gin to die but he didn't want to miss his last breath either. Gin stood in the centre of the arena crouching defensively. He shouted at the beast, primal and aggressive, "COME ON!"

Titan charged at him. Gin adjusted his stance, waiting for the creature to reach him. He ducked under the lunging hands, stabbing Titan three times in the side. He jumped out the way of the monster's swinging arm and cleaved the knife across the monster's eyes. Titan thrashed his hands out, his fingers grazing Gin and tripping him up. In anger, Titan raised his hands over his head and slammed them down. Gin pulled himself out the way but Titan's hand crashed down on top of his shin. He bit back a cry as the crowd erupted disorientating the blinded creature.

Ren watched it walk away from Gin to investigate the sound of the spectators. Then something on the floor near Gin caught his eye. He remembered what the announcer spoke about before Gin came out. Now Ren moved, sprinting around the side of the arena. That door in the floor had to lead somewhere and it had to be accessible from somewhere too. He got to the wall containing the corridor Gin would have walked out of. Just as he thought there was a wooden door in the floor, right by the fence. He yanked the door open and climb down the ladder, without thinking, closing the door over the top of him.

The stench hit him first as he reached the end of the ladder. He forced himself to turn around. His back hit the wall when his eyes laid across what was in front of him. Corpses piled up; their dead terrified stares illuminated by the light that shone through the hatch above.

"Titan he's right there, get him!" The announcers voice shouted from overhead. Ren ran over to the hatch, took a deep breath and then moved some of the bodies out of the way. He looked up into the sky above.

"Gin!" Ren shouted out. "Come this way!" He listened but of course Gin didn't respond. Looking up he saw a mechanism. He followed it to a handle on the wall. "I've found the switch; I can open this!" he shouted up to Gin one last time before running to get the handle.

He pulled against it as hard as he could.

"It's stuck." He panicked. He yanked against it again and again until it finally pulled into its downward position. Ren jumped when there was a loud thud behind him. Gin lay in a crumpled pile, writhing in pain. There were shouts and exclamations from above them but Ren didn't hear the words that they said. He fell to his knees and grabbed Gin, pulling him up and close. Gin lent his full weight against Ren. He wrapped one of his arms around Ren, gripping Ren's clothes. Footsteps rattled the floor above them. "We have to go," Gin said, weakly pushing Ren away from the hatch above.

"Right." Ren agreed.

He looked around them to find a door in the corner of the room. Ren walked over to it and pulled and pushed at it. It suddenly jerked open, Ren slipping on the bloody floor a little.

"Come on, Gin." Ren ran back over to him. He grabbed Gin's arm and pulled him off the floor. Gin fell against him when he tried putting weight on his surely broken leg.

"Careful, Gin! Rest all your weight on me." Ren braced himself as they began to walk away. Light filled the room as the hatch Ren came down opened. Ren dragged Gin towards the next room. He slammed the door shut behind them. Gin jerked out of his grip and pulled a heavy wooden cage down in front of the door. Ren grabbed his sides, stopping him from falling over with it. Ren put Gin's arm over his shoulders again. They turned together and Gin instinctively pulled Ren closer.

Cages lined the walls of the dim room, metal and wooden. Each filled with mutants. Some growled and lunged at the bars as Ren and Gin passed, others sat in the corners of their prisons wailing.

"We're not safe here, Ren," Gin mumbled, leaning on Ren a little harder.

"We'll find a way out," Ren said. They reached another door. Together they listened. "I don't trust this," Ren said. Gin's face was tense.

"Wait," Gin said as Ren reached for the door handle. "Open the cages."

"Are you mad?" Ren whispered harshly.

"Just the calm ones, they'll overrun the place when they smell the people. That'll distract them enough for us to get out," Gin justified. After staring at Gin for a minute, Ren did as he was told, opening the cages furthest away first. Once the last one was open he ran back to Gin, helping him out of the room.

No one was out there. The hall was silent and it was quiet in the arena above as well. "We've gotta get out of here before those mutants get the idea to leave," Gin said. They hobbled down the hall together and reached a stairway. Gin hopped up it one by one, trying his best not to pull Ren about too much.

It opened into the arena again. It was completely empty.

"What the hell happened here?" Ren asked.

Gin pointed to the scattered and broken fence panels. "Looks like the big guy got fed up when his prey left and started biting the hand that fed him."

"Let's hope we don't bump into him, unless you don't mind going round two with him?" Ren smiled.

Gin huffed a small laugh which turned into a coughing fit. "Well, I do have another leg." Gin returned his smile. Gin pointed towards another hallway leading under the seats. There were hundreds of dusty footprints running down the hall.

"I think we're going the right way," Ren said. "But I don't actually know."

"You had one job, Ren. Find the way out," Gin joked.

"Yeah, well if you hadn't gotten hauled off so dramatically, we might have been able to discuss a plan."

Ren bit back just as sarcastically.

Gin's soft smile slipped from his face. "Sorry, if I scared you," he said quietly.

"Stop apologizing, please."

"I will, when you start following my orders."

"What like 'leave me here to die' yeah that's not going to happen."

"Guess, we're at a stalemate then." Gin's little smile returned. He knocked his head against Ren's gently. Ren lent into it.

The halls on this side were as maze-like. They could hear crying and screaming further down the hall. They walked past an open door, there were empty racks and cupboards on the walls. The only thing left behind was a single rifle on its hook and a handful of Blue Bolts lay on the side. Gin was looking at the floor; the footprints were a mess of people running back and forth from the room.

"I think our plan is working," Gin said. "Let's go, there's gotta be a door to the outside somewhere around here."

The shouts got louder as a door came into sight.

"Please let this be an exit, I might pass out if it's not," Gin murmured.

"You pass out on me and I am going to leave you behind." Ren scowled at him.

"Finally."

"I hate you."

They reached the door, the shouts muffled behind it. Ren looked to Gin once before opening it.

The light blinded them for a brief moment when they opened the door. Complete chaos reigned outside. A massive group of Mutants had descended onto the base. Blue bolts flashed and guns fired. Ren pulled Gin around the edge of the base, trying to stay away from the commotion.

"Those rocks, Ren. We'll climb up on those away from the mutants," Gin shouted over the noise, pointing a little way across the wasteland. Ren nodded and dragged him towards it. Gin forced himself forwards, wincing at the tiny amount of pressure he was putting on his sore leg. Bullets pinged off of the metal beside them, pushing them on quicker. They ignored the screams of the people and the animal growls of the mutants. They had tunnel vision, focusing on their haven in front of them.

There was a ridge on the tall rock just above Gin's head.

"You go," Ren ordered, linking his hands to boost Gin up. Gin grabbed the ledge, pulling himself up a little. Ren grabbed under his foot and pushed him the rest of the way. Gin scrambled over the edge. He offered his hand to Ren but he leapt up and hauled himself on top by himself. Ren panted, laying down beside Gin. Gin followed suit, laying carefully on his back, a weird smile on his face.

"Don't look at me impressed, it's not that high," Ren said.

"I'm impressed because of everything that just happened. You got us out alive." Gin's smile widened.

"Not without you."

"What did I do though? I just got myself hurt and you dragged me out. If you hadn't been there, I would have been dead for sure," Gin explained.

Ren couldn't argue with that. "How did you escape?" Gin asked.

Ren hesitated, "A guard walked in and I..." Ren couldn't say the words. The images flashed in his mind again and tears formed in his eyes.

"It's okay, I shouldn't have asked." Gin reached between them and ran his fingers gently over Ren's arm.

The tears fell from Ren's eyes now as he stared up at the darkening sky. Everything that had just happened, everything that he'd done, rushing to the front of his mind. Gin almost died, he almost died, people had died. Good and bad. Gin grabbed his arm and pulled it, the only offer he needed to roll into Gin's arms. He laid his head against Gin's chest and let the sobs overwhelm him. They were safe here, Gin was alive, he was alive. Gin slid his hand under Ren's head, moving it slightly off of a sore spot on his chest, then he let his fingers card through Ren's soft hair. He lent his head against the top of Ren's, offering his silent presence. He didn't know what to say, nothing would change how Ren was feeling. It had been a long day. They were both tired. Ren's tears subsided and he started fiddling with a long strand of Gin's hair.

"We'll have to see if we can find any landmarks to get home by." Gin broke the silence. "I know this area a little but we've never come this close to their base."

"I hope we can find the way home," Ren said. "Are you going to be able to walk home?" he asked sitting up a bit to look Gin in the eyes.

"I'm gonna have to. Maybe if we splint it, I'll be okay." Gin smiled. "Don't worry about it for now, we'll rest tonight and then we'll figure it out tomorrow."

Ren laid his head back down. "It's gone quiet over there," he said.

Only the wind blew across them now, empty, save for the occasional growl of the mutants.

Ren couldn't bring himself to care about the people that lost their lives over there. They weren't people in his eyes; the mutants were more human than them.

"We didn't get any answers," Ren suddenly thought, "and now they're all dead."

"Someone else will know." Gin tried to be encouraging. "They cover a lot of land and control a lot of clans. One of them will know and one of them will tell us when they realise we've beaten the Raiders."

Ren nodded against his chest. "*She's* all I've got left from before. Even Briggs is gone now." Ren sucked in a harsh breath trying not to cry again.

Gin squeezed him a little tighter. It broke his heart and hurt him, more than the pain in his leg, to know Ren was miserable.

Ren exhaled a long breath. "But we've got the clan, and I've got you, don't I?"

"Always," Gin replied without a second thought. "And we'll all help you as much as we can. You're a part of our little family."

"Thank you."

"S'okay." Gin buried his nose in Ren's hair. "What's she like, if you don't mind me asking?"

Ren smiled, a small sad smile, thinking of his little sister.

"She looks like me but her hair is really long and seriously curly. She's annoying and loud but I loved being around her," Ren explained. "We'd go exploring around the woods behind our nans house. She loved putting her wellies on and exploring. That's why our grandad gave her his compass for her seventh birthday. When all this happened, she actually had a lot of fun, investigating everywhere. She never understood how much danger we were in, I never let her fully understand." Ren fell silent, fearing if he went on, he'd cry again. He was too tired to cry any more today.

"I don't have siblings. I was a terribly spoilt only child." Gin grinned, trying to lighten the mood.

"Is that why you're the clan leader? Because you've got a prince complex and needed to get your way?" Ren smiled at him.

"I don't know what you're talking about. But if you keep that up, I might need my guards to take you to the dungeons." Gin laughed.

They laughed together for a moment again falling into a more comfortable silence. Ren yawned and a shiver ran over his body.

"Sleep a little. We've got to get some energy for the journey tomorrow," Gin said, very tired himself.

"Hmm, good idea," Ren said, letting Gin pull him right against his side.

Chapter 11

Ren jumped awake. He sat up with tears already in his eyes. He hesitated for a second but he needed to wake Gin up. He shook him and Gin's eyes blinked open. He sat up, wide awake when he saw the state Ren was in.

"What's happened? Are you okay?" he asked, resting his hand on Ren's cheek.

"I heard him. I heard Briggs barking in my dream." Ren broke down crying. "I can't believe he's gone! I didn't even get to say good bye."

Gin pulled him into his chest, his own feelings of sorrow settling over him as he tried to console Ren.

In the distance, a bark echoed across the wasteland. Ren gasped and sat up, staring into the darkness. "Either I'm going insane or I can hear your dreams as well," Gin said, looking around.

Ren stood, walking to the edge of the rock. He put his hand to his lips and let out a sharp whistle. A series of barks replied. Gin looked towards the sound. West of their position, Gin could just see a group of dim torch lights. They swayed on their steady approach.

"No way." Gin couldn't stop the grin from forming on his face. Ren whistled again and again the barks responded.

"BRIGGS!" Ren yelled into the darkness. The barks continued, steadily getting closer. The torch lights started waving more as they approached, faster. A short figure approached their position, the barking with it. Ren could recognise those striking white flashes anywhere.

He cried out and jumped down off of the rock, stumbling on his bad leg and falling to the dirt. He had just climbed back to his feet only to get bowled back down by the excitable dog.

"Briggs!" Ren cried as he scrubbed his hands through the dog's fur. Briggs licked over his face, Ren laughing at him. He leapt off of Ren and span round in tight circles, his curly tail wagging furiously. He fell onto his side in Ren's lap, panting happily, his tongue hanging from the side of his mouth. Ren was breathless from laughing at his dog's mad behaviour. Briggs turned his head towards the group running towards them.

Ru and a small group of the Opal Fox clan came to a panting stop. "Ren," Ru said, hobbling heavily towards him.

"Are you okay? Where's Gin?" He crouched down beside Ren, placing his hand on the boy's shoulder.

"I'm up here, you old fool," Gin shouted from on top of the rock.

"Gin!" Ru called, pushing himself up using his knee. "What on earth has happened to you two?"

"He got kidnapped," Ren said, still fussing Briggs on the floor.

"And I almost got eaten by a mutant," Gin added with a smug grin on his face. "I've also broken my leg and got blown up."

Ru stared up at him in disbelief. "I'm too old to be dealing with you. We need to get you two back to the base. Where are the Raiders?" Ru said finally, looking over towards the ruins of the base.

"We think most have probably been massacred by the

mutants that they kept caged up for fighting," Gin answered.

"I'm not even going to ask about that right now." Ru pinched the bridge of his nose. "Okay, Riza, take a search party through the Raider base and look for any survivors we can get information from. Kill any mutants you find or fall back if there are too many to handle," he said turning to a tall blonde scout. She nodded to him and led a few of the clansmen towards the ransacked Raider base.

Gin shuffled towards the edge of the rock, lowering his broken leg down. Ru went over to inspect it. "What in fresh hell did this to you?" Ru asked, carefully looking at the damage.

"A massive mutant crushed it. It seriously hurts," Gin spoke softly.

"Yeah, I bet." Ru shook his head. "You're useless when you go off on your own."

"I know." Gin scrubbed his hand over the back of his neck. "Let's get you back."

Some of the clansmen helped lower Gin down from the ledge.

"Let's go home, Briggs." Ren hugged him close and then pushed him off. He stood up and dusted himself off, following behind the group of clan members, Ru leading the way back home. He just hoped that home wasn't too far away.

***

Ren didn't realise how thankful he was to be sleeping in a bed. They'd arrived home and after a small meal Ren was taken back to his bed. The moment his head hit the hessian sack mattress he'd been asleep. Even though it was abrasive and hard and the covers and hides were itchy, he couldn't have wanted for anything more in the world.

He wasn't actually sure what time it was when he rose from his sleep. He ached bone deep but his spirits were high. He'd survived. And Gin and Briggs were both safe and within his grasp. Ren carefully got dressed for the day. Silently thanking whoever had left him some clean clothes on the trunk in his room. He looked to Briggs, who wagged his tail gently. He seemed okay in himself but his front paw was sore again. Ren had watched his shoulder bob as they walked back to the base the night before. Apart from a new bald patch between his shoulders, he was fine.

Ren wanted to go find Gin. He hadn't seen him since Ru took him off to get fixed up last night.

He pulled the curtain door open and jumped out of his skin when he saw three figures just to the left. Gus laughed. "Sorry Ren. Didn't mean to make you jump." The scar running through his left eye creased with a wide smile.

"It's okay. You going to see Gin?" Ren asked.

"Yeah, he's called a meeting," Felix explained.

"Can he not just rest for one day?" Ren said as they started down the hall together.

"How are you anyway, little wren bird?" Tally asked, throwing her arm around Ren's shoulders.

"I'm okay, just glad we survived to be honest."

"You must be lucky or something. I would get you to pick some numbers for me if the lottery was still a thing!" Tally grinned. "And who's the bestest tracking dog in the world?" She bent down to fuss Briggs.

"If it weren't for him, we would have had no chance finding you two. The tracks had been completely blown away when we found him laying out there," Gus said over his shoulder.

They reached the end of the hall and Gus cleared his throat. "You in, boss?" he asked aloud.

"Yeah, come on in." Gin's voice emanated from inside. Ren smiled, hearing his voice. At least he was awake. Gus drew back the curtain and held it so they could enter.

Gin was sat up in bed. He had clean bandages wrapped around his chest and a grey hoodie lay over his shoulders. He had a hide over his lap and his leg propped up on some blankets. It had two wooden splints bandaged tightly either side to hold it still. His hair was wet, and fell over one of his shoulders. He looked tired but he smiled when his friends and Ren entered.

"I told you not to wake him up," Gin said to his three scouts.

"He was already up!" Tally said petulantly. "Frit the life out of him when he was leaving his room." She laughed.

"Fair enough then. I was going to tell you this anyway, but in your own time." Gin smiled at Ren.

"Good thing I woke up in time then," Ren said, perching on the edge of Gin's bed.

Briggs strolled in and sniffed at Gin. He patted his bed, allowing the dog to jump up and curl up next to him. Tally crouched on the floor, Gus and Felix leant against a couple of the room's beams awaiting Gin's news.

Gin took a breath and then spoke, "The search party found the Raider leader alive in the base, and we've taken control of her."

Ren's mouth dropped open. Tally and Gus shared a victorious cheer.

"I think with the right type of 'persuasion', she'll tell us what you want to know, Ren," Gin said.

"Oh yeah, I definitely *just* want a talk with her as well," Tally said, a devilish look on her face.

"The whole clan will be in line for a little chat." Gus smirked.

"Are you okay?" Gin asked Ren.

He was staring into space. Ren blinked and looked at Gin. "Yeah, I just can't believe it," Ren replied.

"When I recover a bit more and she's gotten weaker, we'll go ask her some questions. We'll be the first to speak to her," Gin explained more to his clansmen than to Ren. "Go and let the others know, will you?" he said, signalling for the others to leave.

"Hell yeah!" Tally yelled, jumping up.

The three of them strode from the room, a new energy in their stride.

"Are you sure you're okay?" Gin asked when they were alone.

"I'm just…" Ren couldn't think of the right words to say, he was trying not to lie about how he truly felt to Gin any more.

"I know it's a lot." Gin smiled. "The last few days have been a lot."

Gin sheepishly opened his arms and beckoned Ren to him. Ren crawled to the top of the bed and carefully lay next to Gin. They lay quietly until Ren had found the words he wanted to say.

"I want answers, obviously… and I want her to pay but I can't… I can't make myself wish harm on someone," Ren said, his fingers playing with the wet ends of Gin's hair. "I hate them, I hate what they've done. I hate that they hurt you and took Flo but I can't wish pain on anyone." Ren's voice was tight. Gin's hand idly ran through the back of Ren's hair as he listened.

"I know," he said. "You're not like us."

"You're not bad people," Ren said, sitting up to look Gin in the eyes.

"I didn't mean it like that." Gin smiled, bumping his head against Ren's gently. "What I mean is, we knew this life from the moment the bombs dropped. We fought and killed to get where we are. They were all people, but we had to think about the good of the many over the individuals that tried to hurt them." Ren nodded against his chest.

"Obviously, we didn't kill innocent people. Lots of the people we met ended up joining the clan, but there were the few that tried to steal from or hurt us, and we dealt with them," Gin continued.

"I know," Ren said quietly. "It's all just hard to think about."

"Yeah, definitely." Gin pressed a kiss into the top of Ren's hair.

Loud cheers and shouts erupted from down the hall. "Everyone else is happy about the news," Ren muttered.

"Everyone in this base has lost someone or something to the Raiders," Gin said. "Take Felix and Tally. They both lost their partners. Felix's wife had survived with him when they came to us. They were strong and trusted each other completely. Made them a stellar hunting team. Raiders tracked and attacked their scout group. They killed her in front of him and sent him back to us, the only one alive to send a message. He's been quiet ever since, the guilt still bothering him."

"That's sick," Ren said, pushing closer to Gin.

"Tally on the other hand, met her partner here. They were polar opposites. Tally is Tally, loud and boisterous. Cassie was soft and sweet and super shy. She used to help Nadi out in the kitchen and she'd always slip Tally extras because I swear Tally has a bottomless stomach." Gin laughed to himself before his smile fell away again. "One of the earlier trails, between the bases, took us through a nearby town. They ambushed us and once we'd gotten away, we noticed a small group had been split off. We backtracked and they'd been attacked by mutants. Tally seems okay now, but she hasn't forgiven herself or let herself love anyone else. The love they had really was once in a lifetime."

Ren was shocked into silence for a while. "Why do they hate you so much?" he asked

"It's not just us, they robbed and stole from everyone across these lands. We're powerful and if they weaken us, they can take over the land we control," Gin explained, simply.

Ren stroked Briggs's head.

"Jeez, I'm just glad I haven't been wrapped up in all these politics for very long. If you can even call it that any more."

"It's just like the old politics except it's dangerous for the people dealing with it and not only for the people they control." Gin smiled.

"Louder for the people in the back." Gin stifled a yawn.

"I can go," Ren said, quietly.

"No," Gin said, quicker than he intended. "No, you can stay. I actually had a rough night worrying about you." Gin trailed off towards the end of the sentence, looking up at the corner of the room furthest from Ren's gaze.

"I'll stay then." Ren smiled against Gin's skin.

Gin scooted down the bed carefully, Ren moving the

pillows under his leg. He climbed under the covers next to Gin, Briggs finding a new spot curled up behind Ren's legs. They lay, legs entangled and bodies pressed tightly together. Ren wasn't tired, having just woke up but the steady, deep breaths Gin took brought him immense comfort.

The hopelessness of their last situation finally dawning on him. Gin had looked death in the eye and walked backwards out of its skeletal grip. It was strange. This sudden fear of losing Gin. But he didn't care, couldn't be bothered to care anymore. This feeling, right now, was warm and reassuring and he was too damn tired, to fight it.

Chapter 12

Ren was fed up. He sat in the main hall listening to Gin's briefing. He was explaining the situation about the Raiders in further detail, but Ren could see that sitting in his chair was causing Gin pain, yet he'd refused to call the meeting off.

Both Ru and Ren had tried to convince him, but in the end, they were forced to give up. Either they were going to help him to his chair or he was going to hurt himself further by going there by himself.

With everything explained and scouting routes assigned to include scavenging what they could from the Raider's base, the groups of clan members filed out. Only Ru and Ren remained. Ren stayed in his seat on the ground, staring holes in to Gin's face as he confirmed some final details with Ru.

"You'll go as well, won't you, Ren?" He turned to ask him. "What's with the face?"

"You know full well." Ren scowled.

"He's going back to bed before we leave, if you'll help me do a drug run?" Ru said.

"Yeah, I'll help you," Ren said, sweetly to him.

"I know, I know. I'm going back to bed now. Do you trust me to make it back on my own or do you need to escort me?" Gin said to the both of them.

"I'll send Gus to check up on you," Ru said.

"I'm going." Gin stood from his chair and grabbed the crude crutches they'd made for him. They put a lot of strain on his chest, but it hurt less than trying to walk on his leg.

Ren and Ru followed him out of the hall and watched him until he disappeared around a corner on the way to his bedroom.

"He's as stubborn as a mule." Ru shook his head. "Shall we go then?"

"Yeah, ready when you are." Ren smiled.

Ren ran to grab his satchel to take with him before they left. Then, following Ru, they travelled to a new city, nearby. Its tall walls rose on the horizon, a long line of people queuing out the front waiting to get checked for mutations. Ren and Ru joined the back.

"I haven't seen this many people in a city in a long time," Ren said, peering down the long queue of people.

"Swallow's Grove is the most established city in a hundred miles. They're pretty relaxed on security, so watch yourself, pick pockets thrive in cities like this," Ru explained. "One of the main reasons we put our base where it is."

"Briggs won't let anyone near us." Ren patted the dog on the head. He sat beside them panting under the sun.

The guards were efficient and the line went down quickly. One of the guards looked at Ren and Briggs suspiciously but he changed his tone when Ru pulled the green fox head amulet from his robe.

"Eyes and tongue," he said.

Ren pulled off his glasses and stuck out his tongue. They nodded at the two men and allowed them entry. "Have a good visit to Swallow's Grove, Fox Clan," the second guard said as they walked through the open gates.

"What was that?" Ren asked.

"We offer a bit of protection, having our base so close.

We're allowed in with no hassle or questioning. They scratch our back, we scratch theirs, you know," Ru explained.

The life inside the walled city lifted Ren's spirits high. Crowds bustled around the streets, haggling at stalls and buying all kinds of goods from the merchants. There were neatly built streets, divided up by tall buildings.

"Do lots of people live here?" Ren asked, looking up at the washing lines that crossed between the structures above them.

"Of course, providing you have enough goods or services to offer."

"Is it very expensive?"

"Oh definitely. People didn't adjust well to the world we now live in and they would sell their soul to hide behind these walls. The authorities know that," Ru said, turning down a market street. "Obviously, the more amenities, the more expensive it is. Places like North Bridge and the Western Caves are cheaper because they're dead. Many just use them as rest stops on the way to better places," he continued.

Ru pulled a crumpled piece of paper from the belt of his robe. He scanned the stalls looking for the things they needed to pick up.

They got a couple of items they needed and Ren stored them away in his satchel. Ru then led him to a shopfront. He pushed on the door and a little bell jingled above them. A sound that made more happiness swell in Ren's heart.

The shopkeeper sat on a chair behind the counter. He looked about as old as Ru, with his white hair and thick moustache. He was dressed smartly.

"Ru, long time." He smiled warmly as they approached the counter.

"Hello, Charles. Yes, we're back in this base again," he replied, nodding his head towards the man. "You got any of this?" he asked, handing Charles the slip of paper he'd been carrying. Charles held the paper at arm's length, peering down his nose at it for a moment before he wandered off into a door behind the counter. He returned with a handful of small vials filled with different liquids and pills.

"I've none of this," he said pointing to a long name of a medicine Ren would have never been able to pronounce. "But this is just as good. A little weaker so use double, I've chucked in an extra bottle for ya, free of charge of course," he said tapping the lid of a little brown bottle.

"Thank you, Charles," Ru said, pulling a bundle of cash notes from his robe, most of which he handed over to the man.

"Any time, old friend. And who's this?" he asked as Ren packed everything away in his bag.

"This is Ren. Landed on our base after being attacked by the Raiders. Actually, ended up saving young Gin's life very recently."

"Well, I'm glad to hear Gin's still getting himself into trouble." Charles chuckled.

"I wouldn't mind, if it wasn't me fixing him up afterwards." Ru shook his head. "Well, we'll be off. Good to see you, Charles. I hope to see you again."

"Of course, my friend. Give the clan my best," he said, shaking Ru's hand firmly before they left his shop.

"I just have one more thing Gin asked me to get for him," Ru said, "unless you need anything?"

"Everything I need is at the base," Ren replied easily.

"Perfect. One more stop before home then." Ru led them down another stall lined street.

He stopped at a stall covered in gemstones and jewellery. None of which interested Ren. Another stall distracted him, this one covered in many different kinds of fabrics. He dug through a small bin of loose off-cuts, finding the perfect piece; a square of black cotton with a white paisley pattern printed on it. He looked to the bandana tied around Briggs's neck and the one wrapped around his arm, the pattern matching. He smiled and showed it to the elderly women running the stall.

"How much?" he asked politely.

"One silver coin, lad," she said in a soft, wobbly voice. Ren dug around in his pocket and pulled out the loose change; two silver coins and a gold one.

"Here," he said dropping the silver coins into the lady's hand.

"Bless you." She smiled a wide toothless grin.

He folded the fabric carefully, tucked it away in his bag and then turned to find Ru again.

He was stood a respectful distance away. Ren joined his side. "Ready to go?" Ru asked.

"Yep."

"Hopefully, we won't be too late for dinner." Ru looked up to the steadily changing sky.

The journey home was slightly slower, Ru's old bones aching from a day on his feet. But Ren didn't really mind, Ru reminded him of a wise old owl and he enjoyed his company.

"Have you known Charles for long?" he asked, making polite conversation.

"We were friends before the wars. We met up once a month for coffee and cards." A soft smile settled on Ru's features. "I thought the blast would've wiped him clean out, damn near killed me, never mind that old fool. We reconnected when Gin, the first few clan members and I were looking for supplies to start the base."

"Does he live in the city?"

"Yes, he owned a pharmacy before the war and had the good sense to take all his stock with him. Used it as a bargaining tool to get himself a nice spot in the Swallow's Grove. He also studied herbal medicines; he makes a lot of the remedies himself."

"Wow, a smart man then." Ren smiled.

"Most definitely," Ru said, his eyes trained forwards but with a smile on his face.

***

Darkness had almost settled completely when they reached the base again.

"I'm going to give Gin the thing he wanted. You go to the kitchen, there'll be leftovers for you," Ru said, splitting straight off down the hall.

Ren nodded and took himself and Briggs to the kitchen.

Inside, the kitchen was empty, everyone finished dinner long ago and retired to their beds. On the countertop sat two bowls. A small piece of slate in front of them. 'Ren' written on one and 'Ru' written on the other in curly handwriting. Behind Ren's bowl, a bigger slate with a pile of raw meat, at the bottom 'Briggs' was written with a little heart beside it. Ren beamed, placing Briggs's dinner on the floor and leaning on the countertop to eat his. He watched his dog lap at the chunks of meat and lick the slate clean.

Ru hobbled into the room. He pulled a stool from under the counter and slumped down on it. Ren passed him his bowl and spoon.

"Thank you, Ren," Ru said, exhausted from the days trip.

Ren returned a smile. A small silence stretched between them whilst they ate, filled only by the sound of the slate scraping along the floor as Briggs licked it clean.

"Gin wants to speak with the Raider tomorrow. She won't last much longer if he keeps starving her. I'm telling you this because I know what Gin is like. You need to try and get it out of her tomorrow or you won't have another chance. I can't imagine she'll eat, even if we offered it to her," Ru said seriously. Ren stopped eating, losing his appetite.

"I will," he said.

"Maybe try talking to her on your own if you can. Even though you helped destroy her base, she definitely hates Gin more than you." Ru finished up and stood stiffly. "I'll see you in the morning."

"Yeah, see you, Ru," Ren called after him.

Ren gave Briggs his bowl to lick clean then put them in a pile by the sink and picked up a piece of chalk. 'Thanks, Nadi! ~R and B' he jotted on one of the slates.

"Let's go to bed, Brigadier," Ren said through a yawn, leading the dog back to his own room.

Chapter 13

A little noise disturbed his sleep.

"You promised, you'd get up," she said.

Ren dragged the covers higher over his head for another moment before he looked at the little girl peering over the side of his bed. His room was dark, illuminated only by the light coming in his open door.

"You pinky promised," she whispered again.

"I'm getting up." Ren stretched under the covers. "Go get ready."

They dressed quietly so as not to disturb their grandparents. Ren helped her pull on her welly boots and raincoat. She waited by the door; her rucksack thrown over one shoulder. Briggs waited quietly as well, shaking the sleep out of his fur. Ren gathered water and some snacks, packing them in his own satchel before they stepped out into the foggy morning.

The trees had an eerie mist weaving through them, but it didn't bother either of them, this was common for the time of year and they'd grown up most their life in these woods. Ren led the girl to the river that ran through their land.

"Which way to the waterfall?" she asked.

Ren unzipped her backpack and handed her the compass. "Oh yeah!" she shouted.

"We need to follow it east," Ren said, crouching beside her.

"East, east, east!" She sang turning around in the spot trying to figure out the way to go. "That way," she shouted, pointing her stick down the river like an army general. They marched down the river together. She started singing a little song about walking down the river and all the things she could see. She laughed when Briggs waded into the river, almost falling all the way under when he stepped into a deep bit.

The waterfall wasn't massive, or spectacular, but from her small position it seemed huge. She stood on the river's edge, staring up at the water.

"Careful, Flo. Don't get too close to the edge," Ren warned.

"This is beautiful, Ren," a voice said from behind them.

Flo didn't seem to notice it. Ren turned. Gin walked out of the fog. Ren smiled, stepping towards him. Gin grasped his own chest suddenly, his face twisting in pain. Ren's eyes widened as Gin fell to the floor, not moving. Ren ran to his side, his blank stare looking up at him.

"REN!" Flo screamed behind him. The waterfall was gone, the trees and forest replaced by open wasteland. Her face was dirty, tears streaming down it. She screamed silently as she was hauled away on the shoulder of the faceless man.

"Ren." Gin coughed beside him. Ren's head whipped around to look at them both as he was torn in half.

Ren bolted upright in bed, a croaked yell leaving his throat. Noise to his left, a figure, hands on his body. "Hey Ren, I'm here. It's just me," Gin said, a little breathless.

Ren stared at him, shaking in his grip. He let him go when he relaxed a little. Ren wrapped his arms around Gin's neck, burying his face against his shoulder. Gin grabbed him, pulling him into his lap as Ren sobbed. He carefully laid back on Ren's bed, squeezing the boy as tight he could. Briggs crawled up the bed and pushed his nose under Gin's arm. Ren turned his head to look at him, unwrapping one arm to stroke his head. He rolled onto his side and lifted his paw to hold onto Ren's arm. Ren couldn't stop the sad smile from lifting the corners of his lips for a moment. Gin bumped his chin against Ren's head. "You okay?" Gin asked him softly.

"I'm tired, Gin," he replied.

The sorrow in his voice dragged at Gin's heart. "I know," he said.

"I'm tired and scared." Ren sniffled. "What if I never find her?"

"We will."

"What if she'd not even—" Ren couldn't say the words. "Please don't leave me."

"I'm not going to."

"I've been so lost, following scraps of a lead but now I'm so close. I'm so close because of you. You didn't have to, but you helped me get this far. And I can't do it without you anymore." Ren's voice trembled.

Gin's throat tightened and his breathing deepened as he tried to stop himself from crying. He squeezed his eyes tight and he held Ren impossibly closer.

"All I could think about," Gin started, "when the Raiders were leading me away was that I'd never get to see you again. And that… that I hadn't gotten to tell you that I actually love you. I'd never thought about it but on that walk that was *all* I could think about. Ever since you came, I wanted to get to know you, where you'd come from, why, how. You impressed me with your spirit and fight. I was finding any excuse to be around you." Gin took a long shaky breath. "I didn't have the will to fight that thing when it walked out. But then I saw you, saw you'd gotten out and you were alive and I knew I had to survive. I had to fight because I couldn't just leave you there." Gin kissed the top of Ren's head when he snuggled close. "And when we were laying on that rock, looking up at the sky, I could have died a happy man. I could have succumbed to my injuries or burnt under the sun and I would have died happy and without regret."

"Please don't die now though," Ren said quietly, looking up at him.

"No. I've gotta see how this story ends first." Gin grinned at him.

Ren smiled back at him, new tears falling from his eyes.

"Stop your crying now. I don't want you to cry any more," Gin said gently, wiping Ren's tears away.

"Stay here with me," Ren whispered.

Gin nodded and let him go a little so they could climb under the covers together. Gin grabbed under Ren's knee and pulled it across his body, leaving no space between them. Gin winced when Ren bumped his sore leg by accident.

"Sorry." Ren winced too.

"It's okay, it's extra sore from running up here on it." Gin laughed quietly.

"Sorry for waking you up."

"No, you didn't wake me up. I wasn't sleeping too well anyway." Gin smiled at him, kissing his forehead. They stared at each other for a moment. Ren's eyes glanced over Gin's face. Gin placed his hand on Ren's cheek, Ren's own hand wrapping around his wrist. Gin touched their foreheads together and then slowly lent in to kiss Ren. Ren's breath caught when their lips met and he let his eyes gradually slip closed. When they parted, his heart was pounding. They smiled at each other softly and then Ren laid his head back down on Gin's chest. He felt Gin yawn, making him yawn as well. His eyes closed slowly.

"I love you too, Gin, by the way," Ren's soft voice whispered making Gin smile widely.

Chapter 14

"She hasn't got much life in her," Riza told Ru after checking on their Raider prisoner.

"Yes, Gin is going to speak to her today but I haven't seen him yet," Ru explained.

"No, I haven't either. I saw Briggs wandering about without Ren though, maybe he's with him?" she said shrugging her shoulders.

"Thanks, Riza."

"No problem." Riza smiled and went to get on with her next job.

Ru passed the open base doors. Briggs was outside digging a hole. Ru took amusement from watching the dog hunt whatever he'd smelt in the ground. Briggs stood straight and shook himself off. He trotted back into the base, sniffing at the hand Ru offered him. He had mud lining his muzzle just under his eyes. "Where's Ren?" Ru asked the dog.

Briggs turned his head to the side. "Still in bed?" Ru asked.

Briggs started down the hall towards Ren's room. Ru followed behind him slowly. Briggs slipped into Ren's room; Ru continued to Gin's room.

"You in?" he asked at the curtain door. Nobody said anything. He pulled the curtain back to find an empty room.

"I'm here, Ru," Gin said from behind him.

Ru turned to see Gin and Ren emerge from Ren's room.

"I was just coming to ask if you were ready to see the Raider?" Ru explained.

"Yeah, we're ready." Gin nodded.

Together, they walked to the other side of the base. The fabric halls turned into metal ones as they entered the cell area. A couple of doors lined the walls, all having a different padlock securing the door. Ru pulled out a key and unlocked the door at the end of the hall. It squeaked as it opened.

The Raider leader was chained to the wall opposite the door. Her arms shackled to the wall above her, her head hanging low between her shoulders. She weakly lifted her head when the light filled the room. Her hair was stuck to her face but even in her weak state she had a smirk on her face.

"How the tides did turn." She was the first to speak. "Must feel good, ay Gin?"

"Does a little." Gin hobbled in on his crutches with his own grin on his face. "More for the fact that we were in the same position less than a week ago. But of course, my clan isn't sloppy enough to give you the chance to escape."

Her face twisted in anger.

Gin smirked. "Now, we've got some questions for you. Specifically, Ren has." Gin stepped back to let Ren approach.

"And what do you want to know?" She hissed like a snake.

"A Raider group took someone from me and I want to know where she is," Ren said, bravely.

"You'll have to be more specific; we've taken a lot of people prisoner over the years," she said nonchalantly.

"A little girl! She's seven years old, black curly hair! She has blue eyes, and a purple raincoat on! Her hair was in two bunches, with a yellow and a green scrunchie! She's my little sister and you stole her from me! Where is she?" Ren shouted at the woman; his fists balled up at his sides.

The pent-up anger and sadness spilling over. Gin placed his hand on Ren's side, looming over the Raider. "Why would you take a little girl? We were trying to find somewhere safe. Six against one and you took only her," Ren said his anger fading into sorrow.

She looked up at Gin and spat on the floor between them. Gin's fist raised but Ren grabbed his arm before he could bring it down on her face.

"I want to talk to her by myself, Gin," Ren said, pushing gently against his chest.

"Ren, she's dangerous," Gin pleaded with him.

"I'll be fine, you're going to be right outside." Ren smiled. Gin nodded and took himself and Ru out of the room.

"I never thought that Fox could be muzzled," the Raider said when the door closed again, leaving the room lit only by a single candle.

Ren ignored her and sat on the floor in front of her. "This doesn't really have anything to do with him anyway," Ren said.

"And what was that again?"

"Stop playing around."

"Ah yes, your sister, and what if I say I didn't know?" she asked, an eyebrow raised.

"I know you're lying."

"So naïve." She smirked. "You think the world is that simple."

"What leader doesn't know what their scouts are out doing? If they were just rogue and going out killing people they would have killed or taken me too." Ren scowled back at her. "They took only her for a reason."

"Fine," she said, "we got paid a lot of money to find little kiddies for a bigger, meaner clan. I don't know what for. But regardless, if she's not dead already, you'll die trying to get her. You and your precious little Fox." Her voice was dark and sinister.

"What clan?" Ren said, his head reeling. She didn't say anything.

Ren stood up and shouted, "Who are they?"

The door behind Ren burst open, Gin hearing the commotion inside. But he was ignored by Ren. "The Black Ghost clan, and you're insane if you try and pursue them," she spat out finally. "They'll chew you up and spit you out, little boy. I'd give up on her."

"I'll take the risk," Ren growled, turning away from her.

Ru and Gin followed him out of the room. Ren grabbed Gin and pushed his face into his front when the cell door was closed and locked again. Gin petted Ren's hair.

"Do you know that clan?" Ren asked, his eyes closed tight.

"Yes," Gin replied shortly.

"Where are they?" Ren looked up at him expectantly.

"Ren I-I don't—you can't." Gin avoided his gaze.

"I have to."

"They're psychotic, Ren. They're convicts that broke out of a high security prison when the power went out. They're sick and twisted by the old world's standards, never mind this one!" Gin said desperately. "All our bases are so far north to avoid their territory in the south."

Ren stepped out of his grip, looking down at the floor. His face was the saddest Gin had ever seen it; completely dejected.

"I'm going to go stretch Briggs's legs. I'll be back by dinner," Ren said quietly, walking away from them.

"Don't do anything silly, Ren," Gin pleaded.

"You know I won't, Gin," Ren said without turning around.

***

Ren sat against a stump of a dead, fallen tree just south of the base. Briggs was flat out beside him, his head laying on Ren's leg. His face was dry but the pain in his heart hurt more than it ever had before. He stared across the barren wasteland.

"Of course," he said under his breath, "of course I can't have them both. Of course, the clan is evil and deadlier than any other." Ren's head fell back against the wood. "Guess we're on our own again, Briggs," Ren said stroking the dogs head. "Gin can't come. Even if he wasn't injured, he needs to stay with the clan, it'd be unfair to ask that of him." Ren sucked in a harsh breath. "Who knows if I'll even see him again. I could die and he'll never know what happened."

Briggs stood up and licked at Ren's face. Ren wrapped his arms around the dog's neck and buried his face in his fur.

"No," he said, "no, I'm going to go get her, and we're all going to come back." He sighed heavily and let Briggs go. "We should probably go back in. I already know Gin is worrying where we are." Ren stood up and dusted himself off, walking back to the base.

Chapter 15

Gin went looking for Ren after dinner. He'd left him be for the rest of the day, letting Ren figure out his feelings by himself. But now, he was getting worried. He hadn't eaten with the clan at dinner time and no one had seen him about. He was worried he'd go and do something irrational.

He looked around the base then outside of it, finally looking in Ren's room. Gin let out the breath he didn't know he was holding in when he saw Ren sitting on his bed. Gin went to sit quietly on the bed beside him. More relief filled his mind when Ren leant against his shoulder. Gin wrapped his arm around him.

"I hate this," Ren said.

"Yeah. Me too." Gin rested his head against Ren's.

"I have to go."

"I know." Gin nodded. "And I know I can't stop you."

"I don't want to leave, but I have to."

Gin nodded again. "Yeah, and we'll give you all the resources and help we can because I know you won't let me send Gus or Tal with you."

"No, I won't."

Gin fiddled with the material of Ren's hoodie. "So, you'll come back to me, won't you? With or without her, come back to us," he said.

"I will. But if I don't, don't you dare come looking for me. Don't get yourself killed because of me." Ren looked Gin in the eyes.

"Promise me! Promise me you're not going to get yourself killed because of petty revenge."

"I—" Ren cut Gin off by holding up his pinky finger. Gin smiled at him, linking his finger with Ren's. "I promise you; I won't come looking for you if you don't come back."

Ren's smile widened. "Thank you, Gin."

Ren kissed his cheek. Gin gently held Ren's jaw and kissed him on the lips. "Always," he said, then his face lit up. "Oh, I've got something for you."

Gin let go of him, getting up and holding one finger out to tell Ren to wait. He left the room, hobbling as quickly as he could.

He returned after a few minutes. He had a wrap of fabric in his hand. Gin sat beside him again and handed him the fabric. It was a little heavy. Ren unwrapped it carefully.

Inside was a gemstone. Half blue and the other half green, a thin line of white splitting the two colours. It had been carved into the shape of a fox; the fox was curled up in a ball, its fluffy tail laying under its chin. A small, metal loop was threaded through a hole that had been punched in the top. A long, braided leather cord was coiled up under it. Ren held it up by the leather, the light shining through, illuminating every carved detail; the fur of its tail, its content sleeping expression.

"I stayed up late the last couple of nights making it for you. Because, you're one of us," Gin said quietly.

"It's beautiful," Ren said, a little speechless.

"Ru picked it up for me, said it reminded him of your eyes and I couldn't agree more," Gin explained.

Ren handed it to Gin, turning around so he could put it on for him. Gin clasped the amulet shut behind his neck. The light weight of the stone resting on Ren's chest made him smile.

"I've actually got something for you as well," Ren said, getting up to find his satchel. "Close your eyes." Gin raised his eyebrow but did as he was told.

Ren folded the bandana he'd bought at the market into a triangle. Then folded it up multiple times into an inch-thick strip. Ren grabbed Gin's wrist and tied the cloth on like a bracelet. Making sure the point of the triangle was on top and dead centre.

"You can look now," Ren said.

Gin smile reached his eyes when he saw it.

"Something to remind you of me," Ren said. "We've all got one now, you, me, Briggs and Flo."

"Thank you, Ren. I'll never take it off," Gin said.

"And I'll never take mine off." Ren smiled, his fingers seeking the stone hanging around his neck. Gin's hand lifted to his cheek and pulled Ren into a kiss.

"We should probably get some rest. We've got a lot to plan," Gin said. "Care to join me?"

Ren grinned. "Always," he echoed.

"I want to make the most of our time, whilst you're still in my reach." Gin pulled Ren off his bed and led him off to his room.

***

Ren was ready to go far earlier than he wanted to be. It was barely mid-morning and he had finished packing, ready to leave. He sat on the floor with Gin, Ru and Gus, looking over a hand-drawn map. "We've marked the safest route to the rough area of their base. We've never really come close enough to see the base, but it's around this area," Gus explained pointing along the dotted route on the map.

"Should take you about two weeks," Ru said.

"I've marked on the cities and towns that you can stop in and get supplies. There's also a lot of abandoned buildings and old cities that you can stay in as well. You have to make pace every day or you won't get to them before dark," Gus continued.

Ren nodded. "Thanks, Gus."

"Stay safe though, Ren. Come back if you don't think you'll make it," Gus said, very seriously for once.

"I will." Ren smiled at him. Ren folded the map up and packed it into his satchel.

Ru and Gus left quietly, leaving Ren and Gin by themselves for a minute.

Gin had been quiet the whole meeting. He'd been quiet all morning. Getting dressed that morning, Gin kept stealing touches and kisses. He wasn't ready for Ren to leave either and Ren knew that. But it's what had to happen.

"I'm ready, Gin," Ren said, standing up.

Gin just nodded, standing as well. A strange crevice had opened between them. Ren grabbed Gin's hand, it was cold and rough, but it still closed tightly around his. They walked together through the quiet base, Gin limping beside him, having gotten fed up of using the crutches.

The sun shone brightly through the open base doors. Stepping outside, a small group of clan members met them. They smiled towards him as they stepped outside. Ren's hand slipped from Gin's as he went to say good bye.

"You didn't think you were going to get away without saying good bye, did ya?" Gus hollered.

115

"A proper good bye," Tally said, being the first one to pull him into a hug.

Briggs bounded around, getting pets and hugs from everyone as well.

Gus pulled him close. "You come back ta us now," he whispered close to his ear.

"I will," Ren said, feeling his throat tighten.

Ren made sure to say a proper good bye to everyone. Ru had quiet words of wisdom. Felix, soft words of encouragement. Nadi fluttered around him, worrying if he was going to be too cold or hot or hungry. Then there was Gin, standing off to the side. Ren returned to him.

Gin pulled him close, holding him tighter than he ever had before.

"Don't, don't di—be sa—come back. Just please come back," Gin said against the top of Ren's head.

"I will. You keep your promise too." Ren smiled.

"I will."

"I love you, Gin." Ren looked up at him.

"I love you too, Ren." Gin forced himself to smile. Their lips met softly yet briefly.

"You best throw me a party when I get back." Ren grinned at him. Gin laughed bittersweetly.

They let go of each other and stepped away. Ren called Briggs over and dug his sunglasses out of his bag. "See ya then." He smiled at Gin, turning and waving to the others.

"See you soon," Gin said, watching him turn and leave.

Ren smiled down at Briggs as he trotted beside him, trying desperately not to turn and run back into Gin's arms.

Those first few steps hurt the most. Like he was physically tearing a piece of his soul out and leaving it behind at the base, in Gin's hands. It had been months, maybe only weeks, since he met the Opal Foxes but he felt like he'd spent a good part of his life with them. Now, he was wandering the wasteland again, with only Briggs by his side.

That lit a fire underneath him. He was going to get her back and he was going to come back to them.

Chapter 16

He made good time, Gus's words fresh in his mind, as he approached the first landmark on his map. It was another rotting city that the Foxes controlled.

The sun was beginning to fall towards the horizon. Ren picked up the pace, he wanted to make sure he had long found a place for the night before the darkness settled fully. He shook his head, thinking about how soft he'd gotten staying with the Foxes. Then he thought of the sights he'd seen since and decided to go easy on himself.

The buildings towered over them. Ren and Briggs were tiny in the mass of concrete. The wind was cold in the shadowed streets which seemed to have far too much space between the walls. Ren found a street of shopfronts. The clan had given him plenty of food, water and medicine to sustain him for a few days but old habits die hard. Only one caught his eye. It was a book shop. Ren looked to the horizon, it wasn't even sunset yet, he had some time to have a little look.

Ren pushed at the door; it was stiff but not locked. Ren smiled when the delicate scent filled his nose. Tall, dusty bookshelves lined the walls, most of which still full of books. He looked around the dim aisles. Most of the books containing any sort of information about survival were gone, but many of the story books remained. He saw some familiar spines in the back corner. Bold, colourful writing labelled each volume. Ren pulled one down, turning it to the right to look at its front cover. It was a Japanese manga.

One of his favourite series, about a high school volleyball team. He was going to show Flo it when she was a little older. Ren tucked the first volume in his bag.

"Sorry dear author, I would pay for it if money had any value any more," Ren said, looking up to the ceiling of the bookstore.

Ren wandered around the book shop some more, basking in the memories of forgotten days, until he found a door at the back of the shop behind the counter. It led to a set of stairs with another door at the top. Ren climbed the wooden stairs and cracked open the door at the top.

"Hello?" he said and instantly scolded himself. If someone was in there, he'd basically asked to get assaulted.

Luckily, the apartment was empty. The shop owner must have lived up there. Ren followed narrow hallways to a kitchen. Every cupboard was open and empty save some non-food items. Ren guessed the owner had cleared the place out, considering everything else was in good condition. There was a small living room with only the large furniture left behind. Ren hoped they'd evacuated before the bombs hit and they were somewhere safe now.

At the other end of the apartment there was a bedroom with a proper bed in it, as dusty as the book shop below, but it would be good enough for one night's sleep. Ren dropped his satchel and went back to lock the front door.

He looked out the window at the start of the sunset casting long shadows across the streets. Ren shook the duvet cover out; Briggs sneezing when the dust went up his nose. Ren climbed onto the bed and patted it twice, calling Briggs up with him. They shared a meal together before Ren decided to go to sleep.

The emotions of the day had drained his energy. The wound on his leg throbbed a little when he settled down. He pulled up his trouser leg and looked at it in the sun's light. The long red scar wrapped around the back of his calf in thick, deep lines. It reminded him of Gin's chest. The night before, Ren had traced his fingers along the long, risen lines across Gin's chest. Seeing it for the first time without a bandage on.

Ren shook his head; he didn't want to think about Gin or he'd end up turning back now.

***

Ren coughed as he choked on the harsh breath, he'd sucked in. He was sweating and shaking. The images of dark figures dragging Gin and Flo away from him, slowly fading from his mind. The first light of the morning lit the room around him. It took him a minute to get his bearings in the unfamiliar room, to remember why he was there and what he was doing.

Ren fed Briggs and pulled his boots back on. They left then, seeing no reason to stay. No one was downstairs or even out in the city when they left. He reminded himself that the Foxes controlled this city. No one would be stupid enough to try and cause trouble in it. Ren unfolded his map; the next stop was quite a way away. Double checking his compass, he nodded.

"Come on, let's get going, Briggs." Ren patted his dog's head.

By the time the sun had risen to its full height, it was already starting to hurt his eyes. He'd forgotten how harsh the sun was out here. His leg was beginning to complain and his breath was short.

"They couldn't have picked easier places to get to." Ren groaned.

His complaints were quickly forgotten when he heard the growl of a car engine on the wind behind them. He tried not to panic, but he was completely in the open, giving him no place to hide.

They can't have been Raiders, right? Unless the Foxes had missed one or two. The engine drew closer until the cars sped passed them. Ren's head spun when the car stopped just ahead of him. Ren looked up at the cars. They had no obvious marks on them like the Raider's cars. They were open topped and armour plated.

"What are you doing out here by yourself, kid?" the female driver of the first car asked, jumping out of the vehicle.

She strode confidently towards him. She was wearing short shorts, a vest top and short hiking boots. Her hair was shaved leaving only a dark shadow across her entire scalp. She had many belts across her body, most securing some sort of blade.

"I have no business with you," Ren shouted over to them, stopping where he was.

"Of course not, but you've got a pretty stuffed bag there and we wanted to do business with ya." The other driver joined the first, speaking in a strong Irish accent.

He was just barely taller than the woman. He wore a holey vest, and camo trousers that were tucked into a pair of army boots. His hair was blond, long on the top and shaved around the back and sides; the top part was tied back in a tiny bun. He also had a criss-cross of belts with pouches and blades tucked in them.

"I have nothing to trade with you," Ren said, trying to seem braver than he was.

"We don't either, but you could give us ya stuff and we'll leave ya alone," the male driver spoke again. Ren looked between the closer two and the last three just climbing out of the cars. Briggs growled at them, deterring them from advancing.

"I can't give you any of this. I'm on my way somewhere and my clan only gave me enough for this journey." Ren hoped he could convince them to leave him alone on account that none of them had drawn a weapon yet.

"And what clan might that be?" the woman asked.

"The Opal Fox clan," Ren said, a little louder than necessary.

"Nice try, but the Opal Fox clan don't move on their own. They're always in groups. Ya just trying to scare us off." The man scowled at him.

"No, I'm not," Ren said, reaching in his shirt to pull out his amulet.

The group instinctively reached for their weapons, preparing to defend themselves but the woman raised her hand before they could draw. She approached slowly. Ren put his hand down to Briggs, telling him to stay put. She bent to inspect the stone, the light of the sun making it shine brightly. Her face dropped into a strange expression. Regret or depression, maybe? Ren wasn't actually sure.

She stepped back. "He's telling the truth," she called back to her company, the power in her tone lost.

"Oh hell. Oh no. We're dead. If his leader finds out, we're dead," one of the passengers shouted, his hands in his hair.

His hair was long and shaggy looking and dark in colour.

He wore a plain T shirt and black, dusty trousers. He only had a single belt with a single blade.

"Shut up, idiot," another shouted, shoving the man.

They were the smallest out of all of them. Thick black braids stuck out from under a beanie. They wore a leather jacket over a crop top and tight ripped jeans. They had two long, mean looking swords attached to their back.

"I knew we should have dumped you in that toxic lake back there," the last passenger said, leaning against the car.

He looked bored, clearly not fazed by the situation. He had black hair that lay across his forehead in a sweeping fringe. His hands were stuffed in the pockets of his heavy black trench coat. Underneath he wore a plain grey shirt and black pants.

"What can we do to stop ya from having us killed," the male driver asked, scowling at the ground. Ren wasn't going to have them killed, but they didn't know that. He dug the map out of his bag and showed it to them.

"Do you know where this is?" Ren asked, pointing to a little drawing of a house labelled 'Ranch House'. The two drivers inspected the map.

"I can't say we've passed it but I'm not sure," the woman said.

"Well, take me in that direction. Seeing as you've wasted a lot of daylight holding me here," Ren said, trying a little too hard to sound demanding.

"And you won't tell your leader about this?" the man asked.

"Of course. You scratch my back; I won't tell Gin you tried to mug me." Ren smiled sickly sweetly. The drivers looked between each other.

"Fine then, hop in," the woman finally said.

"Ya dog isn't going to attack us now then?" the man asked.

"No, but he does what he needs to do to protect me," Ren warned.

Ren climbed into the front of the woman's car and Briggs jumped into the man's, it having two less people in it. After getting a thumbs up from the man, the woman led the way driving in the direction of the house.

"So, why you out here on your own? The Foxes don't normally travel by themselves as far as I knew," the woman shouted over the sound of the engine.

Ren shouted back, "I had business before I met the Foxes and I'm going to sort it out now."

"What's your business?" the driver asked.

"I need to find my sister," Ren said, looking down at his hands. "The Raiders took her and gave her to the Black Ghost Clan."

"You shouldn't have business with them, kid," she said.

"My name is Ren."

"You shouldn't have business with them, Ren," she corrected herself.

"I don't really have a choice."

The other male passenger leant into the front. "She's probably already gone, man," he said.

"And I'd be the worst big brother in the world if I didn't go look for her though. What if she is still alive?" Ren turned in his seat to scowl at him.

It was the panicky guy from earlier. He received another smack over the head from the other passenger. "I'm just saying it's a suicide mission." The guy tried to defend himself.

"I know," Ren said, turning back to the front. "Gin tried to convince me of that before I left as well. And if he couldn't, *you* certainly won't be able to." He crossed his arms over his chest.

"Why didn't they send someone with you?" the driver spoke up after a moment of silence.

"It's a suicide mission," Ren echoed. "It wasn't their problem before I met them, it's not their problem now. I'm not going to let anyone else get hurt or die over this."

"You've got some brass balls there, Ren." The person in the back grinned, leaning into the front now. "Just don't hurt yourself swinging them around!" they said.

"I don't know about that." Ren smiled a little, then he changed the subject quickly. "Where are you lot from then? You part of a clan?"

"We're the Red Rams!" the man in the back proclaimed.

"Never heard of you, sounds like a football club or something." Ren raised an eyebrow.

"This is us. We started our own clan," the driver elaborated.

"Cool, so you just go around mugging random people you come across?" Ren asked.

"Well, we've been struggling lately. They don't let us in the walled cities, in case we 'cause trouble'," the man in the back grumbled.

"And we get bullied out of any territory by the bigger clans," the person next to him said.

Ren couldn't really respond, there wasn't anything he could do to help. The two in the back bickered about something as fences started flying by them.

Ren's opinion on these people had changed. They were

just trying to survive like everyone else. A small house appeared from behind a broken-down rock wall.

"That's probably it." Ren pointed.

"That didn't take too long," the driver commented.

Both the cars pulled to a stop outside the house. Ren sat for a moment contemplating something, before deciding it would be a good idea. He dug around in his bag and pulled out the small fabric pouch. The foxes had given him some money to buy supplies on the way, too much in his opinion. So, he dug out a few coins and handed them to the driver.

"Thanks for helping me out. I hope you find some land to control." Ren smiled, jumping over the side of the car.

He whistled through his teeth and Briggs came bounding over to him.

"Thanks, Ren! Good luck getting your sister back and I hope we see you again sometime!" the person stood and shouted in the back, waving their hand high over their head. He turned and waved back, watching as the cars pulled away.

Ren turned back to enter the house. He listened for a minute before going inside. Gus said that they used this house as storage sometimes if they'd come across a particularly good find, so no one should be in there. He checked around the cottage regardless.

It was cold and empty. The stone floors, low ceilings and exposed beams made this place seem homely even though it must have been deserted for years. He would have loved to live in a place like this, surrounded by green fields and forests again. He hadn't seen a green blade of grass in a long time and probably never would again.

Ren shook his head and made his bed ready for the night. He shared some meat that Nadi packed for them with Briggs.

Once again ignoring the longing in his stomach to turn back. He couldn't, regardless of how much it pained him.

However, the mental pain turned into physical pain in the night as cramps twisted in the Blue Bolt scar on his leg. Ru had warned him of this and had given him medicine to combat it but it didn't help.

With only minutes of sleep in his system, he tried leaving the next day. Tears stung his eyes when he forced himself to turn back to the house, the pain too much for him to bear.

He collapsed in the corner of the room, hugging his knees and clenching his teeth as another wave of pain radiated through his body.

Was this really the end? After all this, was he now going to have to give up because of a stupid injury? Ren's head fell back against the wall. He was quiet. He'd failed and he was alone. A new wave of sadness bit at his soul. What if he couldn't get back to Gin? Even if he decided to go back to the clan, would he make it? He thought of the Red Ram Clan and silently begged for them to come back. Even after he'd told them he was going to do this on his own.

Ren scrubbed his hands over his eyes and scowled at himself. He was being ridiculous. This wasn't the end of the world. What was he going to do, just lay there until death claimed him?

Stupid, he thought to himself.

He made his bed again and laid down. He was going to give it one more night before he decided which way to continue. Hopefully with some rest his mind would be clear and rational.

***

Even though his sleep was fitful, Ren had gotten much more rest than the night before. It was still dark when Briggs woke him by leaving his side. He watched Briggs wander towards the door in the moonlight. Ren bolted up when he heard footsteps outside the door. Sweat beaded on his forehead.

Briggs let out a low quiet growl. Ren panicked feeling for the knife in his pocket. But it wasn't there.

He swore under his breath and reached for his bag. He'd gotten too used to the comfort of the Foxes and forgotten basic survival instincts.

His fingers just grazed the hilt of the blade when the door cracked open. Briggs's hair stood high off of his back and when the door swung open his demeanour changed. The figure in the doorway cried out when Briggs jumped up at him, but the sound subsided into laughter.

With his heart in his throat, Ren squinted towards the door. He was sure he imagined that voice. The man closed the door and the moon from the window opposite finally illuminated his face. Ren lunged across the room at him, knocking the crouched man to the floor. His head span with emotion when Gin's arms closed around his tired body. He laughed quietly between the soft kisses he planted against Ren's hair.

"I wasn't expecting this reaction," Gin said with a smile. "Thought you'd be mad."

Ren shook his head against Gin's shoulder. "I told you not to come after me though."

"No, you said 'don't get yourself killed because of petty revenge'. I don't need to get revenge if I come with you to stop you from getting killed in the first place," Gin said in his usual smartass way. "Plus, Ru said and I quote 'I'd rather you go after him and die than mope around like this for the rest of your life'." Gin badly imitated Ru's wobbly voice, making a laugh rise from Ren.

"Classic Ru," Ren said.

"He's right though. I'd rather die at your side than live the rest of my life knowing you died alone."

"Shut up, please." Ren laughed.

Gin smiled against the side of his head.

The world had felt like it was collapsing in on Ren just hours ago but now a calm settled over him. And he realised that he really couldn't be without this man any more.

Chapter 17

They spent the night in each other's embrace and Ren woke up pressed tightly into Gin's side. It was Briggs that pulled him from his sleep, a gentle paw tapped on his side. Ren ignored him but another tap came and another. Ren swung his hand back, gently smacking the dog's chest only to get swatted back twice as hard, claws and all.

Gin laughed making Ren open his eyes and look up at him.

"I think he wants to go out," he said to Ren, reaching over to stroke Briggs's head. Ren pulled himself out of Gin's grip and let Briggs outside, returning to Gin's side.

"We've got a lot of ground to cover," Gin said, making no attempt to get up himself though. "How's your leg today?" Gin asked after Ren had told him last night, the reason why he hadn't made as much progress as he'd hoped.

"It's actually a lot better. Hopefully, that doesn't come back." He smiled.

They finally willed themselves off the floor and started packing for their journey. Ren was folding up his blanket when Gin pulled him into a crouch, out of sight of the window. Gin was staring into space, listening. Ren could hear it too, an engine.

"Wait I think—" Gin shushed Ren when he tried to talk.

The engines came closer until they stopped right outside the house. Gin unsheathed the blade at his hip and stood behind the door.

"Hello again, puppy!" an excited voice called from outside.

Ren sighed with relief and opened the door. Gin protested but Ren ignored him as he went outside to greet the Red Rams again. The small person in the beanie was sat on the floor cuddling Briggs. "Some guard dog you are, Briggs," Ren called over to him.

"We're best friends, he wouldn't bark at us," they said cuddling around his neck tightly.

"Now don't ya go saying anything that'll make me regret coming back to help ya," the male driver said.

Ren smiled. "I wouldn't do that. But you really don't need to."

"Like we said, it's a suicide mission and letting you go do that by yourself just didn't sit right with any of us," the other driver said.

"Plus, if we help you, you might be able to put a good word in for us to your Fox Leader," the panicky passenger spoke up.

"Why would he need to put in a good word to me?" Gin stepped out of the house and joined Ren.

"AH! He's here!" The man gasped, choking on his own breath, causing a coughing fit. The final passenger, the bored looking guy rolled his eyes, slapping him on the back a few times.

"You know these people, Ren?" Gin asked.

"Yeah, they're the Red Rams; they drove me over here the other day," he said, leaving out the whole mugging incident.

The female driver stepped forwards. "I'm Cali." She offered Gin her hand. "This is Miles." She gestured to the other driver. "And this is Lev, Caine and Soule." Cali pointed to the person in the beanie, the guy still having a coughing fit and the one helping him through it.

"Nice to meet you, I'm Gin." He took her hand and shook it firmly. "And you really want to help us?"

"It's better than just driving around aimlessly," Lev said, jumping off the floor and dusting themself off.

"So, where're we headin'?" Miles asked.

Ren pulled out his map and the Rams gathered around him. He pointed out where they were and where they needed to go.

"Why is your trail so wiggly?" Lev asked.

"It's the safest route, it keeps him securely in our territory. We wanted him to get there with the least amount of trouble," Gin explained.

"Well, if we go as the crow flies, we'll get there in one maybe two days," Miles said.

"And if we stop here." Cali pointed out the last landmark on Ren's map. "We can rest up and finalise a plan before going in."

"I believe we store supplies in that city, so we can pick those up and refuel," Soule added.

"Perfect, you ready to go then?" Cali asked Ren.

"Yeah, we'll just grab our stuff from inside." He smiled at her.

Gin followed Ren back inside the house.

"Are you sure we can trust them?" Gin asked in a hushed tone.

"Yeah, for sure."

"How do you know?" Gin wasn't convinced.

"Because when they found me, they were going to mug

me, but I showed them the amulet and told them you'd come for them if you found out they'd hurt me. So, they drove me here in exchange for me not saying anything but now they've actually come back to help. They had their opportunity to run for the hills or just kill me. They aren't bad people," Ren explained.

He shoved the rest of his things in his bag and left Gin to work over that information in silence.

Ren wandered over to the vehicles, Gin leaving the house a few strides behind him. Miles and Soule lifted Briggs into the back of their car with Caine. Lev and Cali were sat waiting in the other one. Ren climbed into the front passenger seat, leaving Gin the other seat in the back. Cali pulled open the glove box in front of Ren and dug around for some sunglasses. "Ready?" Miles shouted over to them.

Cali gave him a thumbs up, starting her engine. Ren watched as the little house disappeared into the distance as they drove away. Apprehension still filled his stomach but it was followed closely by hope.

Chapter 18

Miles had been right. Sunset was steadily approaching as the cars tore towards the abandoned city. "What are we picking up from here?" Ren asked.

"We've got some food, water and a little bit of fuel stashed away in one of the buildings," Cali explained.

"Are you sure it'll still be there?" Gin asked, leaning into the front.

"I mean, if anyone finds it then they were one lucky fella or they watched us hide it." Lev grinned.

"We're not stupid," Cali said, not turning away from the road ahead of them.

Instead of driving directly inside they skirted around the perimeter. Lev stood up in the back, their hands shielding their eyes from the sun, looking into the city.

"Looking clear?" Cali asked.

"Yeah, I think so," Lev said. "SOULE! Clear for you?" They shouted over to the other car.

He turned and gave Lev a thumbs up. The drivers exchanged a look before driving between the rotting buildings. They slowed, the sound of their engines echoing off the walls. Lev, Soule and Caine stayed on high alert. Even though it looked clear from the outside, someone could still be hiding down the streets. They slowed enough for Caine to jump off of the back of Miles's car. He ran along a high wall to a metal, double gate. With a look over his shoulder he jiggled the padlock off the gates and swung them both open.

A school stood tall in front of them as they drove through the gates. Most of the windows were broken and spray-paint covered the majority of its walls. Caine ran up behind them after closing the gates again, hopping onto the back of Cali's car.

"Ay! You didn't fall off this time," Lev teased.

"Ha, ha, you're funny, that was very funny!" Caine said, sarcastically.

"I'll push you off!" Lev scowled.

"Lev," Cali warned.

"We're not even going that fast. He'll only break his ankle or something." They just grinned back.

They drove around the back of the building and parked the cars. They were concealed in the shadows of the school and the half standing perimeter wall.

"Let's go get our shit!" Lev called jumping out the back of the car. They stretched their arms over their head and groaned.

"Be quiet, Lev! We don't know it's completely clear," Cali called after them.

Ren stroked Briggs's head when he came bounding over to them. Gin landed next to him and stumbled a little.

"You okay?" Ren asked, grabbing his forearms to steady him.

"Yeah, leg still isn't hundred per cent." Gin smiled at him.

Ren nodded looking down at the wooden splint bandaged to the outside of Gin's pants. "Doesn't help that the suspension sucks in these," he said tapping the side of the car.

"Hey!" Cali shouted over to them, "this old work horse has gone through the war, literally. Cut it some slack."

"Yeah Gin, I think you would have died in the wasteland before we made it here." Ren grinned up at him.

The Rams led Ren and Gin into the back of the building. It was dark and silent inside. The old building was cold and their footsteps echoed off the walls around them. Wind blew through the broken windows, dirt and sand covering the floors. Sunlight poured into the halls, deepening the shadows around them.

Gin's hand rested against the small of Ren's back. Briggs led the way, nose to the ground sniffing in all of the corners.

His head shot into the air suddenly. Ren stopped dead, searching for what Briggs had seen. He bounded forward twice, skidding on the tile floor. His back legs slid out from underneath him and he fell over. A small, mouse-like creature skittered along the floor, disappearing into a hole in the wall. Briggs stood up and trotted over to the hole, shoving his nose into it.

"You're not a hunter, are ya?" Miles said, "I'm guessing ya didn't rely on him to catch ya dinner, did ya Ren?"

"It's not your fault those little mice are so annoying," Ren said ruffling the dog's ears when he trotted back to them.

"He's pretty good at catching baddies." Gin smiled, patting Briggs's head as well.

"Yeah, scared Caine silly when we first met. He's scary when he gets his teeth out." Lev laughed. Caine tried to protest but his entire clan piled on the teasing.

They climbed a set of stairs, leading them onto an open floor. Lockers lined the walls; classroom doors open in between them. Ren looked over the walls above the lockers. Work by the school children covered them. Ren skimmed over a couple of the pieces. They were written by the kids on their first year of high school, about what they wanted to do once they left the school. So many dreams and ambitions.

Ren's heart ached and he quickly brushed away a tear. He wondered where these kids were. If they were alive with their family, or if they were alone somewhere out there. Ren hoped that wasn't the case. No child should have to live in a world as nightmarish as this.

The group had crossed the space and entered one of the classrooms. Gin was lingering outside the door, waiting for Ren. Ren joined him and they entered the room together. Lev was knelt on a tall metal cabinet. They pushed one of the ceiling tiles up and clambered into the hole.

"You get it now, when they said someone would have to be seriously lucky to have found this stuff," Cali said, turning to Gin.

Gin nodded, a little impressed.

Lev passed little packages down from the ceiling, wrapped in old newspapers. They climbed down after lowering two big, red fuel cans down as well. They carefully replaced the ceiling tile before jumping off the cabinet.

"How's it looking up there?" Cali asked.

"We've got two more cans of fuel and tons of food and water," Lev explained.

"Maybe we could have a feast once we get your sister back." Caine grinned at Ren.

A low growl stopped Ren from replying. Briggs was staring at the wall beneath a window. Ren approached it, everyone in the room silent. Through a broken-down part of the perimeter wall, Ren could see a black car parked behind it. It was in near perfect condition, all the body work looked original. Some people climbed out of it. They were all wearing black cloaks and had guns holstered on their backs, proper guns from wars before.

"That's them," Gin whispered, coming to the other side of the window. "The Black Ghosts."

"They're here?" Caine whispered harshly.

The Rams crouched down, hiding from the view of the window.

"I don't think they're coming over here," Gin said. "They're going into the building next door."

"What are we going to do?" Lev whispered.

"Simple. We stay here until they've gone," Miles said.

"What if they find the cars?" Cali asked.

"Then they take them. We can't risk going out there," Gin answered her.

"But that's all we've got!" Cali said harshly.

"No, your life is all you've got. Everything else is a bonus," Gin snapped back.

"Then what? We'll just wander the wasteland forever after you're done with us!"

"Shush, Cali." Miles scolded her.

"We can't, Miles," she begged.

"Look, we need to trust Gin. This is way bigger than anything we've dealt with!" He cut her off.

Ren and Gin joined the Rams on the floor.

"I can bet your cars aren't as fast as theirs and we have no chance fighting them. It'll be dark soon, so we'll be fighting them and mutants," Gin said frankly.

The Rams were quiet.

"I know you've probably fought very hard for what you've got and if they take them, we'll help you. Trust me, my clan and I are already eternally grateful for the help you've given us," Gin said.

Ren smiled at him.

"We'll trust you then," Lev said, finally breaking the silence.

"Yes, thank you, Gin," Miles said.

Cali nodded as well.

"We may as well stay here for the night then," Soule said. The Rams agreed.

Caine grabbed an armful of the newspaper packages, handing them around to everyone. They were neatly folded and secured with a scruffy piece of twine. Ren unwrapped his; there was a bottle of water and a tin of cooked potatoes inside. Ren grimaced ever so slightly at the can. He'd gotten so accustomed to warm, freshly cooked meals that he'd forgotten that food was food, regardless. Ren and Gin picked a few pieces out of their tins for Briggs. Ren remembered the meat packed away in his bag and he thought about sharing it around as well. He looked around for it.

"Oh no!" He gasped.

"What? What's wrong?" Gin asked, grabbing Ren's arm out of instinct.

"My bag, it's in the car. If they take it, I'll lose Flo's compass," Ren said, a quiet melancholy settling over him.

Gin offered a sympathetic smile, "Well, you'll have her back soon, so um…" Gin stumbled over his words, not really sure what to say to make it better.

"Yeah, I know. I know," Ren said, fiddling with the string in his lap.

Night had settled completely when the engines of the Black Ghosts's car bounced around the city walls. Soule crept to the window and watched them leave. Miles snuck out the room and crossed the hall, tracking the cars until they were far out of sight.

"Cars are safe." Miles smiled when he returned.

"Should we get some stuff out of them. It might get cold in here soon?" Caine asked.

"Yeah, but we need to watch out for mutants now." Cali groaned.

"Why don't only a couple of us go?" Gin suggested.

"And who do you propose stays behind?" Ren said, raising an eyebrow at him.

"Well, maybe you and—"

"I'm not staying behind whilst you go and get eaten." Ren cut him off.

"It will probably be better if only a couple people go. You know quick in and out," Caine said.

"You're just saying that because you don't want to go out in the dark!" Lev teased.

"No! I think Gin is right," Caine snapped back.

"Stop your bickering!" Cali's voice rose above them all, "Me and Gin will go. Then Gin and Caine are happy. He's right, if there are mutants lurking about, they'll be attracted to all of us fumbling around out there. Agreed?"

"I mean, no, but I know better than to argue with ya." Miles sighed.

"No." Ren scowled.

"Well tough, six beats one," Cali said, standing up.

"We'll be fine, Ren. I promise," Gin said, wrapping his hand around the back of Ren's neck, pulling him forward gently to place a soft kiss on his forehead.

"I'm gonna be so mad if you're not," Ren muttered, leaning into Gin for a moment.

Cali and Gin dusted themselves off and silently left the room. Ren huffed, crossing his arms over his chest as he settled back on the floor.

"Ah, so that's why he's so protective over ya." Miles smirked at Ren.

"Huh?" Ren turned to him.

"You two are… ya know," Miles said interlocking his fingers.

"Yeah, I guess," Ren said shrugging.

"Did you get special treatment then, when you were living with the clan?" Soule raised an eyebrow.

"Not really, we haven't really been together that long. We got close after being captured by the Raiders," Ren said

"Ya got caught by the Raiders and are alive to tell the tale?" Miles's eyes went wide.

"Yeah, we ended up destroying their whole base," Ren said, nonchalantly.

"Woah! No way. You've gotta tell us that story," Lev said, lunging forwards onto their hands.

Ren sighed; he'd told this story many times to different clansmen but he supposed it would stop him from worrying about Gin.

***

Gin and Cali traversed the halls. It was pitch black but still and quiet. They listened before turning the corners, in case anything had followed them in.

As they reached the south side of the building the moon illuminated their path. They relaxed a little now they could see what was in front of them.

"So, you and Ren met after the wars?" Cali asked conversationally.

"Yeah, we did," Gin said.

"You seem really close."

"We are."

"It's just you don't seem like the type," she said.

Gin shot her a funny look. "And what exactly is 'the type'?"

She looked over to him shocked and then, realising her mistake, shrugged it off. "Touché."

"To be honest, if we'd met before we probably wouldn't have had anything to do with each other, you know," Gin continued.

"Yeah, this whole thing has pushed unlikely people together," Cali said. "It probably says something about human nature and our need to be around others but I can't be bothered to be philosophical right now."

Gin huffed a laugh in response.

"How did you two come across each other then?" Cali pried some more.

"He was chased down by some Raiders, got licked by a Blue Bolt and ended up crashing through the base's ceiling. But he still managed to give me a headache when he was dragged before me not even two days later." Gin smiled as he recalled Ren's fierce expression when they'd first met.

He looked over to Cali who had a knowing smirk on her face. "Love at first sight, was it?" she asked, smugly.

"No, it wasn't like that." Gin frowned rubbing the back of his neck with his hand.

"Yeah, yeah sure. I believe you." Cali sarcastically agreed.

"Obviously, he was of interest to me. No one just survives travelling that far on their own, you know." Gin trailed off, flustered and defensive.

"Whatever. It's nice you've found someone," Cali said as they approached the door to the outside.

A silence fell between them as they reached for the door. Cali pushed it open gently. She stared into the darkness outside, looking for any tiny movements.

No footsteps. No heavy, laboured breathing.

She pushed the door open fully, flinching as it creaked a little. But it remained silent outside. They left the sanctuary of the school building together. Instinctively, staying side by side. Their eyes began to adjust and the shadows of the cars came into view. They only then left each other's side to collect the things out of the car.

Gin felt his way to the passenger's side and dug around in the foot well until his fingers found the fabric of Ren's bag. He threw the strap over his shoulder and joined Cali at the back of the car. They took all they needed for the night.

"Got everything?" Cali asked, but Gin didn't respond. "Gin?"

"I hear something," he whispered. Cali held her breath to listen. Rubble fell. A scuffed footstep. A low moan.

"It's on the other side," Cali whispered, finally.

"Go slow," Gin said, taking hold of her wrist gently.

They tip toed around the edges of the cars and back towards the looming school building. It was hard to listen for footsteps above the wheezing of the monster. They both held their breath, neither sure of how close it could actually be.

Cali stumbled on some rubble, Gin instinctively stopping her from hitting the floor. The creature screeched.

"Move!" Gin shouted.

The sound of bricks hitting the ground rang out as the creature clawed its way through the perimeter wall. Gin pulled Cali towards the still open building door. Gin's leg failed underneath him as the creature burst through onto their side. His head collided with the wall beside the door. Cali hauled him in and slammed the door shut, resting all her weight against it. Growls and grunts came from underneath the door, but the mutant didn't attempt to follow them.

When she heard the sounds of it walking away, Cali stood up straight again and took her slightly trembling hands off the door.

Gin was sat on the floor rubbing his forehead with one hand and clutching his sore leg with the other. Cali crouched in front of him so she could actually see his face a little.

"You okay?" she asked.

"Yeah, I only hit my head a little," he said, even though he could feel the blood running down his face.

"What happened? That little mutant make you lose your cool?" She grinned, trying to lift their spirits.

Gin laughed. "Nah, I injured myself just before I left to catch up with Ren, hence why I didn't come in the first place. Really shouldn't be running on it."

"Ah, well let's get back before you hurt yourself any more," Cali said, helping him off the ground and carrying another one of the bags, so he didn't have to.

Gin groaned quietly when he put weight on his already painful leg. "Yeah, Ren's going to be even more mad now though." He smiled to himself.

***

"Woah... That's so cool!" Caine said, his mouth wide open.

"I can't believe you two managed to get away with all that," Soule added.

"I think a lot of it was sheer dumb luck, if I'm honest." Ren shrugged.

"But you pulled it off anyway!" Lev cheered, pumping their fist in the air.

"So, what's your plan now?" Miles asked.

Ren went quiet, the smile slipping from his face.

What was his plan? He'd been so focused on finding where they'd taken Flo that he hadn't thought of what to do when he actually found her.

A blood curdling screech spooked them all. Briggs jumped off the ground, barking. Ren was convinced he'd heard Gin shout.

"They're in trouble!" he shouted, scrambling off the floor and running for the door.

"Don't get ya'self killed!" Miles shouted after him, all of the Rams getting up to follow.

Ren grabbed Brigg's bandana, the dog pulling him towards the ruckus.

"Find Gin!" he whispered to him sharply. Ren quickened his pace as a familiar anxiety bubbled in his stomach. They ran down some stairs together. He rounded another dark corner and smashed into something solid. Ren yelped as he hit the floor.

"Ren!" Gin said, breathless.

The moon peeked out from behind the clouds and lit up the hallway. Briggs's tail wagged when Gin's figure became visible.

"What are you doing?" he asked, offering his hands to help Ren off the floor.

"I heard a mutant. I thought you were in trouble," Ren said, shaking slightly now the adrenaline started to leave his body.

"In here?"

"No, outside. I swore I heard you shout. I thought you were in trouble," Ren explained. Gin pulled him close, containing the trembles in his arms.

Miles appeared breathless at the bottom of the stairs. When he saw the three of them safe, he swatted his hand through the air and bent over to catch his breath. The other three Rams reaching their floor as well. "Jeez, Ren!" Lev shouted. "That wasn't very nice! Running off on your own like that."

"Yeah, with the only one of us who can actually see in the dark." Caine gestured to Briggs, wagging his tail at everyone.

"Sorry," Ren muttered.

"It's fine. We're all here and intact, right?" Miles said.

"Yeah, Gin hit his head earlier but we're okay," Cali answered.

"Fine, let's go back. Together," Miles said pointedly.

With Ren and Briggs leading the way they finally made it back to the room.

Soule took one of the bags, digging around for a little oil lamp and matches. Its soft glow bathed the ragged team in light.

Ren gasped when he finally saw the wound on Gin's head. He grabbed his satchel, finding a scrap of fabric inside. He took his water bottle and soaked the fabric. Carefully, he pushed the little baby hair away from the tacky wound and gently dabbed the cloth to it.

"It's just a small graze, Ren," Gin said softly.

"Things like this get worse." Ren protested.

"I promise, I'm fine." Gin offered Ren a smile but the crease in his forehead didn't leave.

"But what if you have concussion. You might be completely incapacitated tomorrow." Ren stopped cleaning to look Gin in the eyes.

"Please don't worry," Gin said, but Ren just looked down at the now bloody rag in his hand.

He unfolded it and balled it back up again, his hands trembling. Gin lifted his chin, both hands holding either side of his face. The corners of Ren's mouth dragged down and his eyes glossed over with tears. Gin sucked in a hard breath. He pulled Ren's head to him with one hand, the other wrapping underneath him to pull him securely into his lap; Ren's legs straddling his own. He pushed his cheek to the side of Ren's head and closed his eyes for a moment, centering himself. Ren's hand slipped underneath the metal protecting Gin's back, screwing tightly into the fabric of his shirt.

"I don't know where to go from here, Gin," Ren barely whispered.

Gin smiled against Ren's hair. "Well, it's a good thing that I've got a plan then."

Ren lifted his head, his face wet and flushed. Gin wiped his thumbs over his cheeks, holding Ren's face gently.

"See, bet you're glad I followed you all the way out here." Gin smiled at him, placing a small kiss on the tiny smile appearing on Ren's lips.

"A plan?" Miles asked.

The Red Rams having been sitting quietly, letting the pair

have their time.

"Yeah, a very loose one," Gin said, relaxing his grip on Ren so he could leave if he wanted. He didn't.

"I think, with there only being a few of us, we can go in quietly. Get lost in the crowd. But it all depends on how the base is built up, how many guards there are and so on."

"You're proposing we just…walk in?" Cali asked, grimacing at him.

"Well, at our base, you could just walk in the front door. Not that anyone would be crazy enough to do that," Gin said.

"Exactly!" Caine cried, his chest rising and falling quickly.

"Exactly…" Gin smirked at them.

Realisation dawned on their faces.

"You're actually insane, Fox," Miles said, shaking his head but not being able to shake the forming smile.

"Foxes are cunning after all!" Lev grinned.

"It is a starting point." Cali sighed, rubbing her forehead. "But we're not going to sleep until we've thrashed this out a little. You might be crazy but I certainly am not!"

The group sat together, until deep into the night, working through scenarios and solutions until they all agreed on an outline of a plan. None of them had come across the Black Ghost's base so all of this needed to be adapted, but for now they had the next step forwards.

Ren was still a little apprehensive when their conversation concluded and they all settled down for the night. He lay awake on his side, pulled close to Gin's front. His hand stroking Briggs's fur gently. This plan was insane, but so was everything else he'd done.

He put his trust in Gin because Gin was prepared to follow him to his death; the least he could do was the same.

Chapter 19

The Black Ghost's base wasn't that difficult to find. They'd woken up early, none of them really sleeping properly and after an hour or two of driving they'd found it. The Rams knew roughly where it was but hadn't dared go near it.

It was obnoxious. Standing tall in the middle of nowhere, like most things did. It had flag poles dotted along the very top. The black fabric flapping in the wind with a menacing grim reaper painted in white on each. It was small however, taking up not even a quarter of the space that the Opal Fox base did.

"I can't see any guards," Ren shouted over the growl of the engine. In fact, he couldn't see anyone, it looked completely dead.

They circled around it, keeping their distance to not rouse suspicion. They parked behind a formation of rocks around a mile away from the base. Gin and Briggs jumped out of Cali's car, swapping with Lev and Soule.

They'd agreed to fly by a couple times to scout it out, leaving Gin behind both times in case he was recognised. Cali took them slightly closer.

"There's no windows," Lev called to the others, their hands shading their eyes from the sun. "And only a front gate." Cali growled.

"Where's all the people?" Ren asked.

"Maybe the clan is smaller than we thought? But even so

we would have seen someone by now!" Lev said.

They circled back to their hiding space. Soule hopped into Miles's car with Caine and left again.

"What'd you see?" Gin asked them.

"There's one entrance and we're certainly not just walking in." Cali sighed, leaning heavily on her steering wheel.

"Maybe they're not here," Lev said. "I didn't see any cars."

"Nah, if I was them, I'd build something to park them in inside," Cali said. "Those gates are definitely big enough to drive a car through."

Miles's car returned. Soule slumped back against the back seat.

"We didn't see anything other than that front gate," he said, defeated. "It's too risky to just drive up to it." Miles sighed.

The group commented weakly about what they could do but Ren had stopped listening. Noise and thought had consumed his mind. He felt his vision tightening as his head started to spin. "...Ren?" Gin's voice filtered through his mind.

His hand was gripping Ren's shoulder and he was bent into his line of sight. The group was silent, looking on at him.

"You all need to leave," Ren said, his eyes open and unfocused.

"What?" Cali frowned slightly.

"All of you need to go. This is stupid and you're going to get killed," he said with more force this time.

"We've come all this way, by our own choice and we're not going to just leave now," Lev said.

"You've come all this way to die! We've come all this way

to die..." Ren's voice faded away.

Ren looked at them all. Each had their own version of a stubborn scowl. And Gin, Gin was wearing that face that Ren had seen many times. He made that face when he was hearing someone out, knowing full well he wasn't going to do what they said.

But then Caine spoke up, shocking everyone into a different kind of silence.

"I mean, even if we did stroll in the front door, we'd still have a good chance because there's only a few of them, right?"

"Huh?" Gin said after he'd gotten over his shock.

"When wo were in one of the towns nearby, I was sneaki—uh, I mean, wandering around and I heard some people—"

"Get on with it!" Miles snapped.

"UH! They said that their numbers had dwindled and that they were relieved because they would stop bothering the town," Caine explained quickly.

"So, why are they such a threat then?" Ren asked, frowning.

"Because there was a rumour that they were escaped convicts. But what if it was just a rumour and the sheer fear of that made them out to be something they're not?" Soule added, "Have any of us actually got first-hand experience with them?"

"But the Raider leader said they were the worst!" Ren said, trying to wrap his head around everything.

"She wasn't exactly a credible source, Ren," Gin said.

"Wait stop!" Miles said, scrubbing his forehead. "You've been sitting on this information, this whole time. And ya didn't think ta say anything!"

"I-I assumed you knew! I mean, I'm terrified still. I don't

want to face one of them never mind a whole group of them!"
Caine cowered away from him.

"Not even when we were discussing the plan last night?"
Miles's frustration simmered away to sheer amazement.

"I don't know." Caine hid his face in his hands.

"You are really stupid." Soule shook his head, but a smile
started on his lips.

"Yeah, like really, really dumb, Caine!" Lev laughed.

"Wait! You're sure about this?" Ren said.

"Yeah, one thing about Caine is he's great at earwigging.
He's stumbled across a lot of helpful information when he's
snooping around places." Cali grinned.

"And you're sure it wasn't just townspeople gossip?" Gin
asked, still a little sceptical.

"Well, I'd like to think that one of the town guards wasn't
lying to the mayor himself," Caine said.

"...How did ya...? Ya know what? I don't care. My mind
can't take ya any more." Miles sat looking like he was going
to lose his sanity.

Lev burst out laughing, keeling over holding their
stomach. A weight lifted from the entire group. Ren smiled, a
laugh bubbling from inside him as well.

"I have an idea. But Cali isn't going to like it," Gin said.
Cali eyed him. "What do you mean by that?"

***

The cars raced full speed towards the Black Ghost base. Ren
could see the dark scowl on Cali's face from his seat in Miles's
car.

She said that, if this was to be the end of her precious

vehicle, she was going to do it by herself.

The rest of them were crammed in the back of Miles's vehicle as they ate up the dusty ground in front of them. Cali pulled ahead, her hands gripping the wheel tightly. Ren's heart pounded as he watched her head straight for the front gate of the base. She slammed on her breaks, taking some of the force away from the engine as it smashed into the gates. Metal crumpled down into the bonnet of the car as it disappeared into the base. Miles skidded to a stop, the back of his car sliding around until they were parallel to the base.

A tense moment passed before Cali's car backed out of the base slowly, dragging the gate out a little way as well. She parked the car beside the base and jumped out, running towards Miles's car.

"Clear!" she shouted.

Everyone else sprang into action, getting out of the vehicle and rushing through the front gate. Each armed with a sword or blade. Cali lingered outside long enough to watch the smoke start to rise out the bonnet of her car. She moped and sighed, running to catch up with everyone inside.

The group stood inside, in a defensive huddle; their weapons held in front of them.

It was gloomy and deafeningly quiet. They were inside some sort of garage. The cars they'd spotted when they were in the school were parked right in front of them.

There was a door to their left. Gin tip-toed over to it, the blood pumping in his ears as he tried to listen for any kind of threats.

Carefully he cracked open the door and peaked out into the hallway. It was empty, burning torches on the walls lighting the long hall.

"Clear," he whispered to the rest of the group. He led them out.

In the very corner of the hall was a hatch like door in the ground and squinting up the corridor, Ren could see a ladder.

"Up or down?" Gin asked.

"I'd assume up," Ren said.

"Should we check down first?" Cali asked. Ren and Gin shared a look. Ren nodded.

Gin pulled the hatch open and recoiled at the scent that hit him. "Whatever is down here has been long dead," he said.

Ren grabbed a torch off the wall as Gin descended. Ren followed him, telling the others to keep watch. Briggs whined, pacing about the hatch as Ren disappeared beyond his reach.

Ren looked up at Gin standing stock still when he reached the bottom of the ladder, his breathing heavy and his eyes wide open.

Ren sucked in a sharp breath, heaving at the sight and smell. He grabbed Gin's arm reflexively. The torch light stretched around them, illuminating the cages. Each filled with corpses and bones.

"You okay down there?" Soule whispered loudly, but neither could answer.

Ren sheathed his weapon and Gin took the torch from him, together they stepped forwards. Gin shined his light into each cage. His throat voided of moisture as he realised the bodies were all tiny. The clothes they wore, the bright colours now dulled by blood and dirt. Ren's hands trembled as they clutched Gin's arm. His head spun.

Then he saw it.

Falling to a crouch and covering his eyes, he inaudibly cried, "No. No. No." In between ragged breaths. But the image remained as if he was still staring at it. The purple raincoat. Her patchy black hair. The pink bandana now looped around rotting bones. He jammed his fists into his eyes, scratched at his face, pulled his hair. Tears flooded down his face and vomit rose in his throat. He fell onto his knees, his hands barely catching him. The floor was sticky and he pulled a hand away like he'd been burnt only to see it was black with congealed blood. He threw up. Tears and mucus dripped from his face as he stared at the floor dry heaving.

Gin was knelt beside him, clutching him, trying to pull him close. He bent over, placing his forehead to Ren's shoulder. Shouts and sobs racked Ren's broken body; his soul aching. He looked back at her.

Curled up on her side in the corner. Her arms tightly held to her chest. Cold and lonely. Ren sobbed again, his eyes slipping closed.

Gin grabbed Ren's chest. He pulled him up and into himself, physically wrapping Ren's arms around his body. Ren sobbed against his shoulder, his tears soaking Gin's shirt. Gin's hands ran over Ren's body, unsure of what to do with himself as tears fell from his own eyes. His heart ached with every painful cry Ren let out.

Ren's breathing changed from unstable sobs to steadily quickening deep breaths. He suddenly let go of Gin and stood up, snatching up the torch that had been abandoned beside them. Gin scrambled to follow him, seeing the twisted scowl on Ren's face.

"I'm gonna kill them!" Ren said, striding back to the ladder.

"Ren, wait a minute," Gin called after him but it was fruitless.

Ren climbed the ladder and pushed passed the waiting Rams. He ignored Briggs when he snuffled in his hand, happy to see he'd emerged from the hatch alive.

"Ren, stop!" Gin ordered.

The group followed quickly behind Ren. He reached the ladder and climbed it. "Stop!" Gin was forced to shout.

Ren was at the top of the ladder before he could reach him. Once he climbed it himself, Gin ran to catch Ren. Grabbing his arm and spinning him around. Ren smacked Gin's hand away and went to walk away again.

"Stop it!" Gin growled at him, grabbing both his arms and holding him tight.

"I'm going to kill them! Don't stop me, Gin!" Ren yelled, disregarding where they were.

"Stop! Stop!" Gin demanded when Ren tried to squirm out of his grip. "Listen to me for a second!" Ren stopped moving and locked Gin with a scowl.

"Ren, you're going to die if you keep running around this place by yourself! And I'll be damned if I'm about to let that happen to you." Gin fixed him with a scowl of his own. "I know you're angry and distraught but letting your emotions blindly lead you to death is just plain stupid." Gin's words were harsh but his tone remained soft as it always was when he spoke to Ren. "You're not a killer."

Ren broke eye contact, his gaze turning to the ground.

"I want them to pay." He whimpered, the anger leaving him weak suddenly.

"We'll make them pay. All of us." Gin nodded towards the Red Rams standing silently behind them. Gin's hands moved to Ren's cheeks. "But you have to go on, for *her* to survive."

That broke Ren again. He wrapped his hands around Gin's

neck. Gin pulled him close and squeezed him for a moment.

"Come on," Gin whispered in his ear, planting a kiss on his cheek and pulling away.

Gin grabbed Ren's hand so he couldn't run off again and turned to the others. They had a shared look of determination on their faces. Briggs wandered up to Ren, sensing his change in mood. Miles had carried him over his shoulders to get him up the ladder. Ren stroked his head, the dog leaning into his hand.

The group looked out ahead of them, the corridor turned a corner at the end. They started down it slowly together. All of them silent once again. Just as they were coming up to the corner Gin tensed, stopping Ren in his tracks. Gin stared into the middle distance, listening hard.

Footsteps approached; equally as quiet as they had been.

The group pressed themselves against the wall. Gin let go of Ren's hand, Lev taking hold of his other one and offering him a kind smile when he looked back at them. Cali stepped to the front with Gin, both unsheathing their weapons. Ren's heart thumped harder knowing they were going to attack whoever was coming. Lev squeezed his hand tighter, a silent way of telling him not to move. Ren's hand found Briggs's bandana. He didn't want him interfering by accident.

Ren barely got a look at the two Ghosts as they rounded the corner before Cali and Gin had rushed them. Cali tackled hers to the ground and Gin had the other's arms pinned behind her back. Their blades pressed against their throats.

Miles and Soule ran in, each grabbing the assault rifles the Ghosts had on their backs.

They were dressed in their long black cloaks, the hoods down showing the black paint covering their cheeks.

They squirmed and writhed but stopped when the blades pushed closer to their throats.

"Where's your leader?" Gin growled through his teeth, his tone foreign to Ren, the true anger radiating from him now.

Neither of them spoke. Gin pressed his blade tighter, blood rising and running down the metal. "Speak up!" Cali spat.

The woman Gin was holding thrashed her head about, connecting it with Gin's nose. She pulled a hand free in the scuffle and drew it back to hit Gin. But Briggs was quicker, pulling away from Ren and grabbing the woman's wrist in his jaw. She yelled and kicked her leg out at the dog. Briggs jumped out of the way. He released her arm for a moment before grabbing it again and shaking his head violently. The woman's mouth opened to scream but Miles clamped it shut again, cutting her tongue between her teeth in the process.

"Don't you dare," he threatened. Briggs growling around the Ghost's broken limb.

Cali's captive frantically eyed Briggs and his comrade.

"The room is on the top floor!" he blurted out. "We heard you break down the gate and were sent to find you. They'll kill you! You won't stand a chance once they know what you've done! You're stupid for coming here!" he screamed hysterically at Cali.

"Yeah, I'm sure we are," Cali said coldly, pushing her blade into his throat.

He spluttered and kicked his legs underneath her, grabbing at her arm weakly as blood poured out his neck. He soon stopped. His eyes stared unfocused up at her. Gin's captive panted in his grip.

"Now you're going to take us to your leader. Or you can

join your friend, your choice," Gin said close to her ear.

"Kill me." She growled under Miles's hand.

Gin shrugged. "Fine."

He forced the blade in her throat until her body fell limp in his hands. They let her drop to the floor.

Lev and Caine went to check around the corner, making sure no one had heard the scuffle. Ren leant against the wall to calm his breathing. He'd never seen that side of Gin or that cold monstrous look in his eyes.

He scowled at himself, the image of Flo's body flashing through his mind again. Gin wasn't the monster here.

Gin came to him, hesitantly touching Ren's arm. Ren smiled at him, reassuring him.

With a nod from Caine, they continued forwards, seeing another ladder around the corner. They pushed on confidently now armed with the assault rifles still in the hands of Miles and Soule – being the only two who could handle them properly.

"Can't be much further, given how tall these rooms are." Soule mused while he was waiting his turn to climb the ladder.

"This must be the top level," Lev added.

Sure enough, noises began to emanate down the hall. Laughter and shouts reached their ears. Briggs growled quietly to himself as they stalked forwards. Ren choked on a breath when a set of double doors came into sight. They led into the middle of the building, directly above where they'd crashed in.

"They seem pretty happy, even though their comrades haven't come back yet," Cali muttered under her breath.

The group surrounded the doors. Miles and Soule stood up front. Caine and Cali behind them. Ren's throat tightened, they hadn't gone over a plan again and he was scared things would go wrong.

Gin squeezed his hand tightly. They shared a look, Gin's confident smile dissipating Ren's fears slightly. He trusted Gin.

Miles took the lead, knocking on the door. The room inside fell silent. He knocked again. Both men either side of the door pointing their guns towards the centre. They waited for whichever door opened first.

It opened and Miles's gun went off. He fell to the metal floor, clutching his shoulder. The man inside cried out too. Soule kicked the doors open and ducked behind the frame.

"Five inside," he called to everyone behind him. Ren dragged Miles to a safer spot as the rest pushed inside, blades drawn. Miles pushed his gun into Ren's hands.

"Cover them!" he ordered.

Ren stared at the very real gun in his hands. "Ren! Go!" Miles shouted.

He took up Miles's place opposite Soule next to the door, looking inside the room.

The others inside were sheltered behind two big metal supporting beams at the edges of the room. The man Miles shot lay dead feet from Soule; another was bleeding out from a long cut across his chest beyond him. The rest of the Ghosts were hiding behind a turned over table towards the back, firing blindly over the top.

Soule shot holes into the wood, hoping to hit one.

"Ren." Miles's hoarse voice made him jump. "Go steady."

Ren looked at him leaning against the wall, hand bloody from clutching at his wound. He looked down at his trembling hands.

A scuffle redirected his attention. His eyes found Caine,

held in Lev's arms, alive but the side of his head was bloody. Cali was kicking a Ghost to the floor, rage covering her expression. He searched for Gin. He was across the room, advancing on one of the men. He stood as tall as Gin and had a long sword in his hand. Gin seemed out matched with his short dagger. Ren's hands stopped trembling, the anger returning inside him.

He lifted the gun to his face.

"Aim careful." Miles's voice drifted into his ears. "Don't shoot any of us."

Ren's finger slipped over the trigger, his eye closing as the other looked down the sight. He squeezed the trigger, the force of it lifting its muzzle into the air.

"Shoulder it!" Miles scolded him. "Shoot in short bursts."

Ren nodded at him, taking up his arms again. He looked across the room in front of him, a woman occupied Cali and Lev, and Gin was handling his one okay. Ren focused on the over turned table. A head peaked up, he aimed and shot. There was a shout and a body fell out to the side of the table, dead.

Caine appeared around the doorway, Soule pulling him to cover. "You okay?" Miles shouted.

"Yeah, pretty sure they sliced my ear off though." Caine offered his friend a pained smile.

"There's only the two and the leader to deal with," Soule said, hesitating to shoot around his comrades. "Forget this," Soule said, throwing his gun in Caine's lap and drawing his sword.

He ran to assist his clansmen. Ren panicked, doing the same when the Black Ghost leader appeared from behind the table to advance on Gin, a knife in hand. Miles grabbed Briggs to stop him from following.

161

Ren sprinted across the room, pulling his blade out. He tackled the larger man before he could reach Gin. They landed with Ren pinned underneath him. Ren sliced his knife blade across the man's dirty face, cutting the corner of his mouth open. The Ghost reeled back in pain. Ren rushed him. His fists slammed into the man's face, blind rage clouding his judgement. His fists burned as bone struck bone. The Ghost leader growled and swung his fist at Ren, knocking him over. He knelt on Ren's chest. A sick grin twisted his face, as he watched the weaker Ren struggle underneath him.

Gin's fist slammed into the Ghost's face. Ren took a second to catch his breath before he ran to help. The Ghost's blade came close to connecting with Ren's face, distracting Gin. Gin turned and grabbed Ren, dragging him out of the way. Ren saw movement behind Gin's back and acting before he registered what it was, he knocked himself into Gin.

White hot pain shocked Ren's body as they hit the floor. The Black Ghost's blade dragging him off of Gin. Gin shielded Ren's body with his own and wrapped his hand around Ren's bleeding arm.

But the man didn't advance. He finally had a moment to look around the room, seeing all of his men downed and the Red Rams advancing ominously.

Miles and Caine entered the room as well, Caine holding Briggs back. The dog growled and barked at the final Ghost.

"Drop your weapon, or I'll let him go," Caine warned. The Ghost stepped back with a defiant scowl on his face.

"Better still, I'll run you through." Cali pointed her weapon at him.

The Ghost relented, throwing his blade at the ground between him and Gin. Lev ran forwards and picked it up.

"You're fools for—" Ren didn't hear any more. Blackness shrouded his mind as he fell limp in Gin's arms.

"Ren!" Gin's voice trickled through the dark. "Open your eyes please!"

Despite the fatigue in his head, he opened his eyes. He was being held tightly in Gin's arms, Gin's concerned face looking down at him. The Rams had gathered around as well.

"Welcome back." Soule smiled; his fingers pushed tight against the pulse on Ren's wrist. "You fainted for a little too long there," Gin said.

Ren nodded at him.

"Do you still feel light-headed?" Soule asked him.

Ren took a minute to figure what exactly he felt. He trembled gently and there was a horrid feeling brewing in the pit of his stomach, but he didn't feel like he'd faint again.

"I think I'm okay," he said finally.

Gin adjusted him and he hissed in pain.

"Sorry! Sorry!" Gin gasped, placing a kiss on Ren's head.

He lent into Gin briefly, letting him know he knew he didn't mean it. He then turned his head slowly to look at his wound. A bloody piece of grey cloth was wrapped uncomfortably tight around his upper arm. He frowned at it and then looked back at Gin, noticing now that the long sleeve of his shirt was missing. "You okay?" Gin asked him quietly.

"Yeah," Ren answered, the sickness subsiding just enough now. Ren gasped. "Where is he?"

"It's fine, Briggs is keeping an eye on him." Cali grinned pointing her thumb over her shoulder.

The Black Ghost leader was sat scowling in the corner, his arms tied securely behind his back. Briggs stood sturdy in front of him, his head low between his shoulders as he stared holes into the man.

"We thought we'd wait for you before we asked him anything," Gin said, softly.

"I don't have anything to say to him," Ren said, his eyes glossed over as he remembered the scene that hid below them. "I just want him dead."

"Please leave that to me," Gin said, resting his forehead against the side of Ren's head whilst fixing the Ghost leader with an evil look. "I've got the perfect idea."

Ren nodded against him. "Will you take me back to her," he whispered. Gin kissed his cheek. "Of course," he said.

Gin lifted Ren off the ground easily. He took him out of the corpse laden room and down to the cellar. The Red Rams dragged the bound Ghost leader behind them.

Gin carefully descended the ladder, Ren holding onto him tightly. Briggs whimpered at the top of the hole again and once they disappeared into the darkness, he jumped in after them.

Gin placed Ren on the floor in front of the cage, lighting a torch and standing off to the side. "Go deal with him," Ren said, staring at her.

"I'll be back in a minute then," Gin said, reluctantly turning away from him.

Briggs sniffed the air towards the cage and let out a low whine. Ren dragged him close, Briggs coming to lay with his head on his lap. No tears ran now. He was too tired, too broken to feel the pain any more.

He blamed himself. He'd failed her. He thought about what he could have done to get here quicker, how he could have prevented this fate. But there was no way.

If he hadn't been injured, he would have continued North. He wouldn't have met Gin and they wouldn't have ended up destroying the Raider's base. He wouldn't have gotten the lead that brought him here. And she'd been gone too long. It wouldn't have mattered if things had gone differently, he would have always been too late.

He heard Gin approach quietly. His boots scuffing along the dirt floor. He came and sat behind Ren, enclosing him in a warm, strong hug. Gin didn't say anything, just laid his head on Ren's shoulder with his eyes closed. Ren let his head fall back against Gin's. Gin's heart thumped against his back, their breathing syncing.

Briggs's head lay heavy in his lap, his cold fur soft under Ren's hand.

He could hear an engine roar upstairs followed by a triumphant cry from the Red Rams.

His thoughts took him to Ru, his kind words and gentle, caring nature.

To Nadi and her miracle way of making horrid ingredients into tasty meals. To Tally, Gus and Felix and their constant bickering.

The Opal Fox clan who had once been strangers to him were now, home.

Ren lifted his head and took a deep breath. Gin looked up at him.

"I found this," he said, opening his hand to show Ren the keys inside. Ren looked down at it.

"Can you get me hers?" he asked quietly, straightening the black bandana on Gin's arm.

Gin nodded against his shoulder and stood up. Ren didn't watch. He didn't want to look at him disturbing her but he was too selfish to leave without something of hers.

Gin returned it to him. It was dull and blacken on one side, covered in blood and tissue. He folded it carefully, the cleaner, pinker side on top before placing it safely in his pocket.

He then stood up. Gin taking his arm to keep him up right. And together they left that horrid place behind.

Outside the Red Rams were gathered around one of the black cars they'd seen earlier. Cali grinned in the driver's seat but it disappeared when she saw Ren and Gin emerge. She turned the engine off and got out, the clan meeting the two of them half way.

"What did you do with him?" Ren asked.

Gin turned him around. Just above the doorway was a small platform.

The ex-clan leader was bound, gagged and stripped naked on top of it. He had some small cuts carved into his chest, thin lines of blood trickling out of them. Enough to attract the flies, birds and hopefully mutants. Ren looked over him, stared into his eyes with an emotionless expression. Ren wanted to make sure that he'd remember his face, because Ren definitely wouldn't be able to forget his.

"Let's go," Ren said, turning away and ignoring the man's muffled cries.

They piled into the two cars; Miles's arm not injured enough to prevent him from driving them back to the base.

They had a long drive, but to Ren it didn't matter. It could have been across the world for all he cared. Gin was right by his side and that would make any distance seem insignificant.

They were going home. Home.

Ren's heart swelled and he lent closer to Gin, letting his eyes slip closed. He liked the sound of Home.

Chapter 20
Epilogue

Ren tucked his laces tightly into the side of his boots and grabbed his metal chest plate. He pulled it on and fumbled with the buckle on the side for a moment. He ran his hand across the fox head on the front, feeling the dents and scrapes where it had protected him in the past.

"You ready to go?" he asked Briggs, who lay sprawled out on their big bed. He jumped up, wagging his tail furiously.

They were running late but he had his excuses. They ran through the busy base together. He returned the cheery expressions of the clan's people they passed. He skidded around the corner and out the front door.

The sun was high and the air was still. He looked over to the two cars parked out front and the small group of Opal Foxes and newly named Opal Rams. The Red Rams had taken the place in the clan that Gin had offered them. Each now having an Opal amulet around their neck of a Ram's head.

He wandered over to them.

"I bet you half my dinner, that I'll take out more mutants than you!" Tally claimed, pointing her finger at Gus.

"Ha! Fine, but you're gonna be hungry tonight!" He laughed at her; his nose high in the air. Miles and Felix shared the same exhausted look behind them.

"Don't worry, I'll share my dinner with you, Tal!" Lev said, cuddling onto Tally's arm. Gus's laughter got louder.

"Even your own lover don't think you'll win!"

"Levy, honey. You're supposed to be on my side." Tally redirected her soft tone to Lev.

"I am! But I've got you're back if you don't win." They grinned back.

Ren couldn't help but smile at them.

A pair of hands on his shoulders distracted him. One slid down to grip his strong bicep, the other staying high, away from the amputated remains of his right arm.

The wound he'd sustained in the fight with the Black Ghosts being too deep and damaging for Ru to save. But with Gin at his side, it was like he never needed it in the first place.

Gin placed a soft kiss on Ren's neck.

"I thought I was going to be the late one, but clearly not." Ren grinned.

Gin's mouth lifted from his skin and then Ren felt him glaring into the side of his head.

"I've got an excuse, what's yours?" Ren turned his head to him, an innocent smile on his face. Gin fixed him with a fake scowl.

Gin's appearance still caught Ren off guard sometimes. After they'd returned, Gus had made him make good on his promise and they'd shaved his hair clean off. Ren liked it now that it was growing back, a thick layer of soft fuzzy hairs covering his head. But he did admit he was sad to see the long hair go.

"Oh, I don't know, maybe being the leader of a clan and having more to do than just get out of bed in the morning. I even woke you up before I left," Gin said, standing straight to cross his arms at Ren.

Ren just grinned at Gin and then pointed down at his

unlaced boots. Gin rolled his eyes but couldn't stop a smile covering his face when he crouched to the ground, as he did every day for Ren.

"You ready to go? Or do you need help getting dressed too?" Gin teased lightly.

"I did it all by myself," Ren answered talking like a child would.

Gin reached for the buckles on Ren's chest plate and tightened them both so it fit his body snuggly. "Yeah, 'all by yourself'." Gin mocked him, turning to the others. "Let's get out of here," he ordered the group.

Ren sat in the back of Cali's newly modified, black car. Squeezed in with Briggs, Tally and Lov; Gin sitting comfortable in front. He looked over to Miles's car pulling up next to them, Soule in the front with him and Caine, Felix and Gus in the back. Gus gestured rudely to Tally when she stuck her tongue out at him. Briggs cutting out their messing by licking Tally's face a little too eagerly. Ren laughed at the chaos in the back seat.

"Ru wants us to stop by the town just beyond Flo's place for some meds," Gin said, business as usual.

"He's making the youngsters do his errands now as well." Ren joked, knowing he'd do literally anything that man asked him to.

Ru was getting on and his limp had worsened. But with good herbal medicines from his pharmacist friend, Charles and the cars to take him and the other older clans people between bases, he was still going strong.

The Opals reached their first stop, the ruins of the manor house. Only Ren, Gin and Briggs jumped out, the rest staying behind quietly. They walked side by side through the remains of the rotting building. Both staying quiet to not disturb any mutants that could have wandered inside.

They emerged out the other side. Descending a set of cracked marble stairs and walking passed an empty water fountain.

There was a marble structure at the bottom of the garden, ivy overgrowing its walls and moss covering the roof. Ren stepped through the empty doorway, ducking under a delicate spiderweb.

In the middle of the building, a square of sunlight shone down to the floor. Gin helped Ren down to the floor, bathing him in soft light. In front of him stood a wooden grave.

A light piece of lumber that Gin had helped him carve after he'd lost his arm. It had a scrolled edge and a fox head carved into the centre at the top. Underneath the fox were the words:

Flo Whittaker Beloved sister of Ren and Gin Reyes.

Ren bowed forwards and touched his forehead to the ground. Beneath his head, in a beautifully carved wooden box, was Flo's pink bandana and her compass that had guided him to her finally.

He sat up and Gin helped him off the ground. Together they stood, basking in the light that shone into the tiny building.

"I've wanted to ask you something this whole year, Ren," Gin said softly, his arm pulling Ren close to his side.

Ren looked up at him.

"Why didn't you want to ask the Ghost leader anything? Why didn't you have anything to say to him?" Ren looked back at his sister's grave.

"Because knowing why wouldn't have changed

anything," he said. "Knowing why she was left like that or why they'd taken her wouldn't have brought her back. It would have just raised more emotions that I'm too tired to deal with any more."

Ren looked up at Gin, a genuine peaceful look on his face. Gin smiled at him and cupped Ren's cheeks, Ren's hands covering them. He bent and kissed Ren softly.

Gin had noticed the change in Ren. Once he was strong enough to leave the base and they built this memorial for Flo, he seemed more at peace. Gin believed that this was the true Ren he was seeing. Closer to the Ren that might have existed before all this had happened. Even though he was now jaded and plagued by nightmares, Gin felt that he was beginning to live his life for himself again. That he was finally free.

They parted but kept their foreheads pressed together.

"I love you, Ren. And I'll always be by your side, in this life and the next," Gin whispered.

Ren smiled. "I love you too. And thank you, I don't think I could live if you weren't beside me." Ren spoke again after a moment of silence, "Shall we go? We've got new land to find."

Gin nodded, letting him go but taking his hand.

Ren turned and waved as they walked away. "We'll see you again soon. Pinky promise!"

Printed in Great Britain
by Amazon

17270134R00100